G.K.CHESTERTON

A MISCELLANY
OF MEN

A MISCELLANY
OF MEN
BY
G. K. CHESTERTON

METHUEN & CO. LTD.
36 ESSEX STREET W.C.
LONDON

CONTENTS

A

MISCELLANY OF MEN

The Poet and the Cheese

There is something creepy in the flat JL Eastern Counties ; a brush of the white feather. There is a stillness, which is rather of the mind than of the bodily senses. Rapid changes and sudden revelations of scenery, even when they are soundless, have something in them analogous to a movement of music, to a crash or a cry. Mountain hamlets spring out on us with a shout like mountain brigands. Comfortable valleys accept us with open arms and warm words, like comfortable innkeepers. But travelling in the great level lands has a curiously still and lonely quality ; lonely even when there are plenty of people on the road and in the market-place. One's voice seems to break an almost elvish silence, and something unreasonably weird in the phrase of the nursery tales, " And he went a

A Miscellany of Men

little farther and came to another place," comes back into the mind.

In some such mood I came along a lean, pale road south of the fens, and found myself in a large, quiet, and seemingly forgotten village. It was one of those places that instantly produce a frame of mind which, it may be, one afterwards decks out with unreal details. I dare say that grass did not really grow in the streets, but I came away with a curious impression that it did. I dare say the market-place was not literally lonely and without sign of life, but it left the vague impression of being so. The place was large and even loose in design, yet it had the air of something hidden away and always overlooked. It seemed shy, like a big yokel; the low roofs seemed to be ducking behind the hedges and railings, and the chimneys holding their breath. I came into it in that dead hour of the afternoon which is neither after lunch nor before tea, nor anything else even on a half-holiday ; and I had a fantastic feeling that I had strayed into a lost and extra hour that is not numbered in the twenty-four.

I entered an inn which stood openly in the market-place yet was almost as private as a private house. Those who talk of " public-

The Poet and the Cheese

houses " as if they were all one problem would have been both puzzled and pleased with such a place. In the front window a stout old lady in black with an elaborate cap sat doing a large piece of needlework. She had a kind of comfortable Puritanism about her ; and might have been (perhaps she was) the original Mrs. Grundy. A little more withdrawn into the parlour sat a tall, strong, and serious girl, with a face of beautiful honesty and a pair of scissors stuck in her belt, doing a small piece of needlework. Two feet behind them sat a hulking labourer with a humorous face like wood painted scarlet, before a huge mug of mild beer which he had not touched and probably would not touch for hours. On the hearthrug there was an equally motionless cat; and on the table a copy of Household Words.

I was conscious of some atmosphere, still and yet bracing, that I had met somewhere in literature. There was poetry in it as well as piety ; and yet it was not poetry after my particular taste. .It was somehow at once solid and airy. Then I remembered that it was the atmosphere in some of Wordsworth's rural poems ; which are full of genuine freshness and wonder, and yet are in some incurable 3

way commonplace. This was strange; for Wordsworth's men were of the rocks and fells, and not of the fenlands or flats. But perhaps it is the clearness of still water and the mirrored skies of meres and pools that produces this crystalline virtue. Perhaps that is why Wordsworth is called a Lake Poet instead of a mountain poet. Perhaps it is the water that does it. Certainly the whole of that town was like a cup of water given at morning.

After a few sentences exchanged at long intervals in the manner of rustic courtesy, I inquired casually what was the name of the town. The old lady answered that its name was Stilton, and composedly continued her needlework. But I had paused with my mug in air, and was gazing at her with a suddenly arrested concern. " I suppose," I said, " that it has nothing to do with the cheese of that name ? " " " Oh yes," she answered, with a staggering indifference, " they used to make it here."

I put down my mug with a gravity far greater than her own. " But this place is a Shrine ! " I said. " Pilgrims should be pouring into it from wherever the English legend has endured alive. There ought to be a colossal statue in the market-place of the man who 4

The Poet and the Cheese

invented Stilton cheese. There ought to be another colossal statue of the first cow who provided the foundations of it. There should be a burnished tablet let into the ground on the spot where some courageous man first ate Stilton cheese, and survived. On the top of a neighbouring hill (if there are any neighbouring hills) there should be a huge model of a Stilton cheese, made of some rich green marble and engraven with some haughty motto: I suggest something like ' Ver non semper viret; sed Stiltonia semper virescit.' ' The old lady said, " Yes, sir," and continued her domestic occupations.

After a strained and emotional silence, I said, " If I take a meal here to-night can you give me any Stilton ? "

" No, sir ; I'm afraid we haven't got any Stilton," said the immovable one, speaking as if it were something thousands of miles away.

" This is awful," I said : for it seemed to me a strange allegory of England as she is now ; this little town that had lost its glory and forgotten, so to speak, the meaning of its own name. And I thought it yet more symbolic because from all that old and full and virile life the great cheese was gone ; and only the beer remained. And even that will be stolen

by the Liberals or adulterated by the Conservatives. Politely disengaging myself, I made my way as quickly as possible to the nearest large, noisy, and nasty town in that neighbourhood, where I sought out the nearest vulgar, tawdry, and avaricious restaurant. There (after trifling with beef, mutton, puddings, pies, and so on) I got a Stilton cheese. I was so much moved by my memories that I wrote a sonnet to the cheese. Some critical friends have hinted to me that my sonnet is not strictly new ; that it contains " echoes " (as they express it) of some other poem that they have read somewhere. Here, at least, are the lines I wrote :—

SONNET TO A STILTON CHEESE

Stilton, thou shouldst be living at this hour. And so thou art. Nor losest grace thereby ; England has need of thee, and so have I— She is a Fen. Far as the eye can scour, League after grassy league .from Lincoln tower To Stilton in the fields, she is a Fen. Yet this high cheese, by choice of fenland men, Like a tall green volcano rose in power.

Plain living and long drinking are no more, And pure religion, reading Household Words,

And sturdy manhood, sitting still all day, Shrink, like this cheese that crumbles to its core ; While my digestion, like the House of Lords, The heaviest burdens on herself doth lay. 6

The Poet and the Cheese

I confess I feel myself as if some literary influence, something that has haunted me, were present in this otherwise original poem; but it is hopeless to disentangle it now.

The Thing *o ^y *o ^y ^ *o

THE wind awoke last night with so noble a violence that it was like the war in heaven ; and I thought for a moment that the Thing had broken free. For wind never seems like empty air. Wind always sounds full and physical, like the big body of something; and I fancied that the Thing itself was walking gigantic along the great roads between the forests of beech.

Let me explain. The vitality and recurrent victory of Christendom have been due to the power of the Thing to break out from time to time from its enveloping words and symbols. Without this power all civilizations tend to perish under a load of language and ritual. One instance of this we hear much in modern discussion : the separation of the form from the spirit of religion. But we hear too little of numberless other cases of the same stiffening and falsification ; we arc far too seldom re-

The Thing

minded that just as church-going is not religion, so reading and writing are not knowledge, and voting is not self-government. It would be easy to find people in the big cities who can read and write quickly enough to be clerks but who are actually ignorant of the daily movements of the sun and moon.

The case of self-government is even more curious, especially as one watches it for the first time in a country district. Self-government arose among men (probably among the primitive men, certainly among the ancients,) out of an idea which seems now too simple to be understood. The notion of self-government was not (as many modern friends and foes of it seem to think) the notion that the ordinary citizen is to be consulted as one consults an Encj^clopscdia. He is not there to be asked a lot of fancy questions, to see how he answers them. He and his fellows arc to be, within reasonable human limits, masters of their own lives. They shall decide whether they shall be men of the oar or the wheel, of the spade or the spear. The men of the valley shall settle whether the valley shall be devastated for coal or covered with corn and vines ; the men of the town shall decide whether it shall be hoary with thatches 9

A Miscellany of Men

or splendid with spires. Of their own nature and instinct they shall gather under a patriarchal chief or debate in a political marketplace. And in case the word " man" be misunderstood, I may remark that in this moral atmosphere, this original soul of self-government, the women always have quite as much influence as the men. But in modern England neither the men nor the women have any influence at all. In this primary matter, the moulding of the landscape, the creation of a mode of life, the people are utterly impotent. They stand and stare at imperial and economic processes going on, as they might stare at the Lord Mayor's Show.

Round about where I live, for instance, two changes are taking place which really affect the land and all things that live on it, whether for good or evil. The first is that the urban civilization (or whatever it is) is advancing ; that the clerks come out in black swarms and the villas advance in red battalions. The other is that the vast estates into which England has long been divided are passing out of the hands of the English gentry into the hands of men who are always upstarts and often actually foreigners.

Now, these are just the sort of things with

The Thing

which self-government was really supposed to grapple. People were supposed to be able to indicate whether they wished to live in town or country, to be represented by a gentleman or a cad. I do not presume to prejudge their decision; perhaps they would prefer the cad ; perhaps he is really preferable. I say that the filling of a man's native sky with smoke or the selling of his roof over his head illustrates the sort of things he ought to have some say in, if he is supposed to be governing himself. But owing to the strange trend of recent society, these enormous earthquakes he has to pass over and treat as private trivialities. In theory the building of a villa is as incidental as the buying of a hat. In reality it is as if all Lancashire were laid waste for deer forests ; or as if all Belgium were flooded by the sea. In theory the sale of a squire's land to a moneylender is a minor and exceptional necessity. In reality it is a thing like a German invasion. Sometimes it is a German invasion.

Upon this helpless populace, gazing at these prodigies and fates, comes round about every five years a thing called a General Election. It is believed by antiquaries to be the remains of some system of self-government ; but it consists solely in asking the citizen questions is

A Miscellany of Men

about everything except what he understands. The examination paper of the Election generally consists of some such queries as these : "I. Are the green biscuits eaten by the peasants of Eastern Lithuania in your opinion fit for human food ? II. Are the religious professions of the President of the Orange Free State hypocritical or sincere ? III. Do you think that the savages in Prusso-Portugucse East Bunyipland are as happy and hygienic as the fortunate savages in Franco-British West Bunyipland ? IV. Did the lost Latin Charter said to have been exacted from Henry III reserve the right of the Crown to create peers ? V. What do you think of what America thinks of what Mr. Roosevelt thinks of what Lord Kitchener thinks of the state of the Nile ? VI. Detect some difference between the two persons in frock-coats placed before you at this election."

Now, it never was supposed in any natural theory of self-government that the ordinary man in my neighbourhood need answer fantastic questions like these. He is a citizen of South Bucks, not an editor of Notes and Queries. He would be, I seriously believe, the best judge of whether farmsteads or factory chimneys should adorn his own sky-line, of

The Thing

whether stupid squires or clever usurers should govern his own village. But these are precisely the things which the oligarchs will not allow him to touch with his finger. Instead, they allow him an Imperial destiny and divine mission to alter, under their guidance, all the things that he knows nothing about. The name of self-government is noisy everywhere : the Thing is throttled.

The wind sang and split the sky like thunder all the night through ; in scraps of sleep it filled my dreams with the divine discordances of martyrdom and revolt; I heard the horn of Roland and the drums of Napoleon and all the tongues of terror with which the Thing has gone forth : the spirit of our race alive. But when I came down in the morning only a branch or two was broken off the tree in my garden ; and none of the great country houses in the neighbourhood were blown down, as would have happened if the Thing had really been abroad.

The Man who Thinks Backwards ^>

THE man who thinks backwards is a very powerful person to-day : indeed, if he is not omnipotent, he is. at least omnipresent. It is he who writes nearly all the learned books and articles, especially of the scientific or sceptical sort; all the articles on Eugenics and Social Evolution and Prison Reform and the Higher Criticism and all the rest of it. But especially it is this strange and tortuous being who does most of the writing about female emancipation and the reconsidering of marriage. For the man who thinks backwards is very frequently a woman.

Thinking backwards is not quite easy to define abstractedly ; and perhaps the simplest method is to take some object, as plain as possible, and from it illustrate the two modes of thought: the right mode in which all real results have been rooted ; the wrong mode, which is confusing all our current discussions, especially our discussions about the relations of the sexes. Casting my eye round the 14

room, I notice an object which is often mentioned in the higher and subtler of these debates about the sexes : I mean a poker. I will take a poker and think about it; first forwards and then backwards, and so, perhaps, show what I mean.

The sage desiring to think well and wisely about a poker will begin somewhat as follows : Among the live creatures that crawl about this star the queerest is the thing called Man. This plucked and plumeless bird, comic and forlorn, is the butt of all the philosophies. He is the only naked animal; and this quality, once, it is said, his glory, is now his shame. He has to go outside himself for everything that he wants. He might almost be considered as an absent-minded person who had gone bathing and left his clothes everywhere, so that he has hung his hat upon the beaver and his coat upon the sheep. The rabbit has white warmth for a waistcoat, and the glow-worm has a lantern for a head. But man has no heat in his hide, and the light in his body is darkness ; and he must look for light and warmth in the wild, cold universe in which he is cast. This is equally true of his soul and of his body ; he is the one creature that has lost his heart as much as he has lost 15

his hide. In a spiritual sense he has taken leave of his senses ; and even in a literal sense he has been unable to keep his hair on. And just as this external need of his has lit in his dark brain the dreadful star called religion, so it has lit in his hand the only adequate symbol of it: I mean the red flower called Fire. Fire, the most magic and startling of all material things, is a thing known only to man and is the expression of his sublime exter-nalism. It embodies all that is human in his hearths and all that is divine on his altars. It is the most human thing in the world ; seen across wastes of marsh or medleys of forest, it is veritably the purple and golden flag of the sons of Eve. But there is about this generous and rejoicing thing an alien and awful quality : the quality of torture. Its presence is life ; its touch is death. Therefore, it is always necessary to have an intermediary between ourselves and this dreadful deity ; to have a priest to intercede for us with the god of life and death ; to send an ambassador to the fire. That priest is the poker. Made of a material more merciless and warlike than the other instruments of domesticity, hammered on the anvil and born itself in the flame, the poker is strong enough to enter the burning 16

fiery furnace, and, like the holy children, not be consumed. In this heroic service it is often battered and twisted, but is the more honourable for it, like any other soldier who has been under fire.

Now all this may sound very fanciful and mystical, but it is the right view of pokers, and no one who takes it will ever go in for any wrong view of pokers, such as using them to beat one's wife or torture one's children, or even (though that is more excusable) to make a policeman jump, as the clown does in the pantomime. He who has thus gone back to the beginning, and seen everything as quaint and new, will always see things in their right order, the one depending on the other in degree of purpose and importance : the poker for the fire and the fire for the man and the man for the glory of God.

This is thinking forwards. Now our modern discussions about everything, Imperialism, Socialism, or Votes for Women, are all entangled in an opposite train of thought, which runs as follows : —

A modern intellectual comes in and sees a poker. He is a positivist ; he will not begin

with any dogmas about the nature of man, or any day-dreams about the mystery of fire. He will begin with what he can see, the poker ; and the first thing he sees about the poker is that it is crooked. He says, " Poor poker ; it's crooked." Then he asks how it came to be crooked ; and is told that there is a thing in the world (with which his temperament has hitherto left him unacquainted), a thing called fire. He points out, very kindly and clearly, how silly it is of people, if they want a straight poker, to put it into a chemical combustion which will very probably heat and warp it. " Let us abolish fire," he says, " arid then we shall have perfectly straight pokers. Why should you want a fire at all ? " They explain to him that a creature called Man wants a fire, because he has no fur or feathers. He gazes dreamily at the embers for a few seconds, and then shakes his head. " I doubt if such an animal is worth preserving," he says. " He must eventually go under in the cosmic struggle when pitted against well-armoured and warmly protected species, who have wings and trunks and spires and scales and horns and shaggy hair. If Man cannot live Avithout these luxuries, you had better abolish Man." At this point, as a rule, the 18

crowd is convinced ; it heaves up all its clubs and axes, and abolishes him. At least, one of him.

Before we begin discussing our various new plans for the people's welfare, let us make a kind of agreement that we will argue in a straightforward way, and not in a tail-foremost way. The typical modern movements may be right; but let them be defended because they are right, not because they are typical modern movements. Let us begin with the actual woman or man in the street, who is cold ; like mankind before the finding of (ire. Do not let us begin with the end of the last red-hot discussion—like the end of a red-hot poker. Imperialism may be right. But if it is right, it is right because England has some divine authority like Israel, or some human authority like Rome ; not because we have saddled ourselves with South Africa, and don't know how to get rid of it. Socialism may be true. But if it is true, it is true because the tribe or the city can really declare all land to be common land, not because Harrod's Stores exist and the commonwealth must copy them. Female suffrage may be just. 19

But if it is just, it is just because women are women, not because women are sweated workers and white slaves and all sorts of things that they ought never to have been. Let not the Imperialist accept a colony because it is there, nor the Suffragist seize a vote because it is lying about, nor the Socialist buy up an industry merely because it is for sale.

Let us ask ourselves first what we really do want, not what recent legal decisions have told us to want, or recent logical philosophies proved that we must want, or recent social prophecies predicted that we shall some day want. If there must be a British Empire, let it be British, and not, in mere panic, American or Prussian. If there ought to be female suffrage, let it be female, and not a mere imitation as coarse as the male blackguard or as dull as the male clerk. If there is to be Socialism, let it be social; that is, as different as possible from all the big commercial departments of to-day. The really good journeyman tailor does not cut his coat according to his cloth ; he asks for more cloth. The really practical statesman docs not fit himself to existing conditions ; he denounces the conditions as unfit. History is like some

deeply planted tree which, though gigantic in girth, tapers away at last into tiny twigs ; and we are in the topmost branches. Each of us is trying to bend the tree by a twig : to alter England through a distant colony, or to capture the State through a small State department, or to destroy all voting through a vote. In all such bewilderment he is wise who resists this temptation of trivial triumph or surrender, and happy (in an echo of the Roman poet) who remembers the roots of things.

The Nameless Man ^ ^ ^ *^

^ I A HERE are only two forms of govcrn-JL ment •— the monarchy or personal government, and the republic or impersonal government. England is not a government; England is an anarchy, because there are so many kings. But there is one real advantage (among many real disadvantages) in the method of abstract democracy, and that is this : that under impersonal government politics are so much more personal. In France and America, where the State is an abstraction, political argument is quite full of human details'—some might even say of inhuman details. But in England, precisely because we are ruled by personages, these personages do not permit personalities. In England names are honoured, and therefore names are suppressed. But in the republics, in France especially, a man can put his enemies' names into his article and his own name at the end of it.

This is the essential condition of such can-dour. If we merely made our anonymous articles more violent, we should be baser than we are now. We should only be arming masked men with daggers instead of cudgels. And I, for one, have always believed in the more general signing of articles, and have signed my own articles on many occasions when, heaven knows, I had little reason to be vain of them. I have heard many arguments for anonymity ; but they all seem to amount to the statement that anonymity is safe, which is just what I complain of. In matters of truth the fact that you don't want to publish something is, nine times out of ten, a proof that you ought to publish it.

But there is one answer to my perpetual plea for a man putting his name to his writing. There is one answer, and there is only one answer, and it is never given. It is that in the modern complexity very often a man's name is almost as false as his pseudonym. The prominent person to-day is eternally trying to lose a name, and to get a title. For instance, we all read with earnestness and patience the pages of the Daily Mail, and there are times when we feel moved to cry, " Bring to us the man who thought these strange thoughts! Pursue him, capture him, take great care of

him. Bring him back to us tenderly, like some precious bale of silk, that we may look upon the face of the man who desires such things to be printed. Let us know his name ; his social and medical pedigree." But in the modern muddle (it might be said) how little should we gain if those frankly fatuous sheets were indeed subscribed by the man who had inspired them. Suppose that after every article stating that the Premier is a piratical Socialist there were printed the simple word " Northcliffe." What does that simple word suggest to the simple soul ? To my simple soul (uninstructed otherwise) it suggests a lofty and lonely crag somewhere in the wintry seas towards the Orkneys or Norway ; and barely clinging to the top of this crag the fortress of some forgotten chieftain. As it happens, of course, I know that the word does not mean this ; it means another Fleet Street journalist like myself, or only different from myself in so far as he has sought to secure money while I have sought to secure a jolly time.

A title does not now even serve as a distinction : it does not distinguish. A coronet is not merely an extinguisher: it is a hiding-place.

The Nameless Man

But the really odd thing is this. This false quality in titles does not merely apply to the new and vulgar titles, but to the old and historic titles also. For hundreds of years titles in England have been essentially unmeaning ; void of that very weak and very human instinct in which titles originated. In essential nonsense of application there is nothing to choose between Northcliffe and Norfolk. The Duke of Norfolk means (as my exquisite and laborious knowledge of Latin informs me) the Leader of Norfolk. It is idle to talk against representative government or for it. All government is representative government until it begins to decay. Unfortunately (as is also evident) all government begins to decay the instant it begins to govern. All aristocrats were first meant as envoys of democracy ; and most envoys of democracy lose no time in becoming aristocrats. By the old essential human notion, the Duke of Norfolk ought simply to be the first or most' manifest of Norfolk men.

I sec growing and filling out before me the image of an actual Duke of Norfolk. For instance, Norfolk men all make their voices run up very high at the end of a sentence.

A Miscellany of Men

The Duke of Norfolk's voice, therefore, ought to end in a perfect shriek. They often (I am told) end sentences with the word " together," entirely irrespective of its meaning. Thus I shall expect the Duke of Norfolk to say : " I beg to second the motion together" ; or " This is a great constitutional question together." I shall expect him to know much about the Broads and the sluggish rivers above them ; to know about the shooting of water-fowl, and not to know too much about anything else. Of mountains he must be wildly and ludicrously ignorant. He must have the freshness of Norfolk, nay, even the flatness of Norfolk. He must remind me of the watery expanses, the great square church towers and the long level sunsets of East England. If he does not do this, I decline to know him.

I need not multiply such cases; the principle applies everywhere. Thus I lose all interest in the Duke of Devonshire unless he can assure me that his soul is filled with that strange warm Puritanism., Puritanism shot with romance, which colours the West Country. He must cat nothing but clotted cream, drink nothing but cider, read nothing but Lorna Doone, and be unacquainted with any town 26

The Nameless Man

larger than Plymouth, which he must regard with some awe, as the Central Babylon of the world. Again, I should expect the Prince of Wales always to be full of the mysticism and dreamy ardour of the Celtic fringe.

Perhaps it may be thought that these demands are a little extreme; and that our fancy is running away with us. Neverthe" less, it is not my Duke of Devonshire who is funny ; but the real Duke of Devonshire. The point is that the scheme of titles is a misfit throughout: hardly anywhere do we find a modern man whose name and rank represent in any way his type, his locality, or his mode of life. As a mere matter of social comedy, the thing is worth noticing. You will meet a man whose name suggests a gouty admiral, and you will find him exactly like a timid organist : you will hear announced the name of a haughty and almost heathen grande dome, and behold the entrance of a nice, smiling Christian cook. These are light complications of the central fact of the falsification of all names and ranks. Our peers are like a party of mediaeval knights who should have exchanged shields, crests, 27

and pennons. For the present rule seems to be that the Duke of Sussex may lawfully own the whole of Essex ; and that the Marquis of Cornwall may own all the hills and valleys so long as they are not Cornish.

The clue to all this tangle is as simple as it is terrible. If England is an aristocracy, England is dying. If this system is the country, as some say, the country is stiffening into more than the pomp and paralysis of China. It is the final sign of imbecility in a people that it calls cats dogs and describes the sun as the moon——and is very particular about the preciseness of these pseudonyms. To be wrong, and to be carefully wrong : that is the definition of decadence. The disease called aphasia, in which people begin by saying tea when they mean coffee, commonly ends in their silence. Silence of this stiff sort is the chief mark of the powerful parts of modern society. They all seem straining to keep things in rather than to let things out. For the kings of finance speechlessness is counted a way of being strong, though it should rather be counted a v> T ay of being sly. To-day the Parliament does not parley any more 28

than the Speaker speaks. Even the newspaper editors and proprietors are more despotic and dangerous by what they do not utter than by what they do. We have all heard the expression " golden silence." The expression " brazen silence " is the only adequate phrase for our editors. If we wake out of this throttled, gaping, and wordless nightmare, we must awake with a yell. The Revolution that releases England from the fixed falsity of its present position will be not less noisy than other revolutions. It will contain, I fear, a great deal of that rude accomplishment described among little boys as " calling names " ; but that will not matter much so long as they are the right names.

The Gardener and the Guinea ^> ^

STRICTLY speaking, there is no such thing as an English Peasant. Indeed, the type can only exist in community, so much does it depend on co-operation and common laws. One must not think primarily of a French Peasant, any more than of a German Measle. The plural of the word is its proper form ; you cannot have a Peasant till you have a peasantry. The essence of the Peasant ideal is equality ; and you cannot be equal all by yourself.

Nevertheless, because human nature always craves and half creates the things necessary to its happiness, there are approximations and suggestions of the possibility of such a race even here. The nearest approach I know to the temper of a Peasant in England is that of the country gardener ; not, of course, the great scientific gardener attached to the great houses ; he is a rich man's servant like any other. I mean the small jobbing gardener who works for two or three moderate-sized 30

gardens ; who works on his own ; who sometimes even owns his house ; and who frequently owns his tools. This kind of man has really some of the characteristics of the true Peasant——especially the characteristics that people don't like. He has none of that irresponsible mirth which is the consolation of most poor men in England. The gardener is even disliked sometimes by the owners of the shrubs and flowers ; because (like Micaiah) he prophesies not good concerning them, but evil. The English gardener is grim, critical, self-respecting ; sometimes even economical. Nor is this (as the reader's lightning wit will flash back at me) merely because the English gardener is always a Scotch gardener. The type does exist in pure South England blood and speech ; I have spoken to the type. I was speaking to the type only the other evening, when a rather odd little incident occurred.

It was one of those wonderful evenings in which the sky was warm and radiant while the earth was still comparatively cold and wet. But it is of the essence of Spring to be unexpected ; as in that heroic and hackneyed line about coming " before the swallow dares." 3'

Spring never is Spring unless it comes too soon. And on a day like that one might pray, without any profanity, that Spring might come on earth, as it was in heaven. The gardener was gardening. I was not gardening. It is needless to explain the causes of this difference ; it would be to tell the tremendous history of two souls. It is needless because there is a more immediate explanation of the case : the gardener and I, if not equal in agreement, were at least equal in difference. It is quite certain that he would not have allowed me to touch the garden if I had gone down on my knees to him. And it is by no means certain that I should have consented to touch the garden if he had gone down on his knees to me. His activity and my idleness, therefore, went on steadily side by side through the long sunset hours.

And all the time I was thinking what a shame it was that he was not sticking his spade into his own garden, instead of mine : he knew about the earth and the underworld of seeds, the resurrection of Spring and the flowers that appear in order like a procession marshalled by a herald. He possessed the garden intellectually and spiritually, while I only possessed it politically. I know more about flowers than coal-owners know about 32

coal; for at least I pay them honour when they are brought above the surface of the earth. I know more about gardens than railway shareholders seem to know about railways : for at least I know that it needs a man to make a garden ; a man whose name is Adam. But as I walked on that grass my ignorance overwhelmed me—and yet that phrase is false, because it suggests something like a storm from the sky above. It is truer to say that my ignorance exploded underneath me, like a mine dug long before ; and indeed it was dug before the beginning of the ages. Green bombs of bulbs and seeds were bursting underneath me everywhere; and, so far as my knowledge went, they had been laid by a conspirator. I trod quite uneasily on this uprush of the earth; the Spring is always only a fruitful earthquake. With the land all alive under me I began to wonder more and more why this man, who had made the garden, did not own the garden. If I stuck a spade into the ground, I should be astonished at what I found there . . . and just as I thought this I saw that the gardener was astonished too.

Just as I was wondering why the man who
used the spade did not profit by the spade,
3

he brought me something he had found actually in my soil. It was a thin worn gold piece of the Georges, of the sort which are called, I believe, Spade Guineas. Anyhow, a piece of gold.

If you do not see the parable as I saw it just then, I doubt if I can explain it just now. He could make a hundred other round yellow fruits : and this flat yellow one is the only sort that I can make. How it came there I have not a notion—unless Edmund Burke dropped it in his hurry to get back to Butler's Court. But there it was : this is a cold recital of facts. There may be a whole pirate's treasure lying under the earth there, for all I know or care ; for there is no interest in a treasure without a Treasure Island to sail to. If there is a treasure it will never be found, for I am not interested in wealth beyond the dreams of avarice-—since I know that avarice has no dreams, but only insomnia. And, for the other party, my gardener would never consent to dig up the garden.

Nevertheless, I was overwhelmed with intellectual emotions when I saw that answer to my question ; the question of why the garden did riot belong to the gardener. No

better epigram could be put in reply than simply putting the Spade Guinea beside the Spade. This was the only underground seed that I could understand. Only by having a little more of that dull, battered yellow substance could I manage to be idle while he was active. I am not altogether idle myself; but the fact remains that the power is in the thin slip of metal we call the Spade Guinea, not in the strong square and curve of metal which we call the Spade. And then I suddenly remembered that as I had found gold on my ground by accident, so richer men in the north and west counties had found coal in their ground, also by accident.

I told the gardener that as he had found the thing he ought to keep it, but that if he cared to sell it to me it could be valued properly, and then sold. He said, at first with characteristic independence, that he would like to keep it. He said it would make a brooch for his wife. But a little later he brought it back to me without explanation. I could not get a ray of light on the reason of his refusal; but he looked lowering and unhappy. Had he some mystical instinct that it is just such accidental and irrational wealth that is the doom of all peasantries ? 35

Perhaps he dimly felt that the boy's pirate tales are true ; and that buried treasure is a thing for robbers and not for producers. Perhaps he thought there was a curse on such capital: on the coal of the coal-owners, on the gold of the gold-seekers. Perhaps there is.

The Voter and the Two Voices ^> *^

THE real evil of our Party System is commonly stated wrong. It was stated wrong by Lord Rosebery, when he said that it prevented the best men from devoting themselves to politics, and that it encouraged a fanatical conflict. I doubt whether the best men ever would devote themselves to politics. The best men devote themselves to pigs and babies and things like that. And as for the fanatical conflict in party politics, I wish there was more of it. The real danger of the two parties with their two policies is that they unduly limit the outlook of the ordinary citizen. They make him barren instead of creative, because he is never allowed to do anything except prefer one existing policy to another. We have not got real Democracy when the decision depends upon the people. We shall have real Democracy when the problem depends upon the people. The ordinary man will decide not only how 37

he will vote, but what he is going to vote about.

It is this which involves some weakness in many current aspirations towards the extension of the suffrage ; I mean that, apart from all questions of abstract justice, it is not the smallness or largeness of the suffrage that is at present the difficulty of Democracy. It is not the quantity of voters, but the quality of the thing they are voting about. A certain alternative is put before them by the powerful houses and the highest political class. Two roads are opened to them ; but they must go down one or the other. They cannot have what they choose, but only which they choose. To follow the process in practice we may put it thus. The Suffragettes-—if one may judge by their frequent ringing of his bell-—want to do something to Mr. Asquith. I have no notion what it is. Let us say (for the sake of argument) that they want to paint him green. We will suppose that it is entirely for that simple purpose that they are always seeking to have private interviews with him ; it seems as profitable as any other end that I can imagine to such an interview. 38

The Voter and the Two Voices

Now, it is possible that the Government of the day might go in for a positive policy of painting Mr. Asquith green ; might give that reform a prominent place in their programme. Then the party in opposition would adopt another policy, not a policy of leaving Mr. Asquith alone (which would be considered dangerously revolutionary), but some alternative course of action, as, for instance, painting him red. Then both sides would fling themselves on the people, they would both cry that the appeal was now to the Caesar of Democracy. A dark and dramatic air of conflict and real crisis would arise on both sides ; arrows of satire would fly and swords of eloquence flame. The Greens would say that Socialists and free lovers might well want to paint Mr. Asquith red ; they wanted to paint the whole town red. Socialists would indignantly reply that Socialism was the reverse of disorder, and that they only wanted to paint Mr. Asquith red so that he might resemble the red pillar-boxes which typified State control. The Greens would passionately deny the charge so often brought against them by the Reds ; they would deny that they wished Mr. Asquith green in order that he might be invisible on the green benches of 39

the Commons, as certain terrified animals take the colour of their environment.

There would be fights in the street perhaps, and abundance of ribbons, flags, and badges, of the two colours. One crowd would sing, "Keep the Red Flag Flying," and the other, " The Wearing of the Green." But when the last effort had been made and the last moment come, when two crowds were waiting in the dark outside the public building to hear the declaration of the poll, then both sides alike would say that it was now for democracy to do exactly what it chose. England herself, lifting her head in awful loneliness and liberty, must speak and pronounce judgment. Yet this might not be exactly true. England herself, lifting her head in awful loneliness and liberty, might really wish Mr. Asquith to be pale blue. The democracy of England in the abstract, if it had been allowed to make up a policy for itself, might have desired him to be black with pink spots. It might even have liked him as he is now. But a huge apparatus of wealth, power, and printed matter has made it practically impossible for them to bring home these other proposals, 40

The Voter and the Two Voices

even if they would really prefer them. No candidates will stand in the spotted interest; for candidates commonly have to produce money either from their own pockets or the party's; and in such circles spots are not worn. No man in the social position of a Cabinet Minister, perhaps, will commit himself to the pale-blue theory of Mr. Asquith ; therefore it cannot be a Government measure, therefore it cannot pass.

Nearly all the great newspapers, both pompous and frivolous, will declare dogmatically day after day, until every one half believes it, that red and green are the only two colours in the paint-box. The Observer will say : " No one who knows the solid framework of politics or the emphatic first principles of an Imperial people can suppose for a moment that there is any possible compromise to be made in such a matter ; we must either fulfil our manifest racial destiny and crown the edifice of ages with the august figure of a Green Premier, or we must abandon our heritage, break our promise to the Empire, fling ourselves into final anarchy, and allow the flaming and demoniac image of a Red Premier to hover over our dissolution and our doom." The Daily Mail will say : " There is no half-41 way house in this matter ; it must be green or red. We wish to see every honest Englishman one colour or the other." And then some funny man in the popular Press will star the sentence with a pun, and say that the Daily Mail liked its readers to be green and its paper to be read. But no one will even dare to whisper that there is such a thing as yellow.

For the purposes of pure logic it is clearer to argue with silly examples than with sensible ones : because silly examples are simple. But I could give many grave and concrete cases of the kind of thing to which I refer. In the later part of the Boer War both parties perpetually insisted in every speech and pamphlet that annexation was inevitable and that it was only a question whether Liberals or Tories should do it. It was not inevitable in the least; it would have been perfectly easy to make peace with the Boers as Christian nations commonly make peace with their conquered enemies. Personally I think that it would have been better for us in the most selfish sense, better for our pocket and prestige, if we had never effected the 42

The Voter and the Two Voices

annexation at all; but that is a matter of opinion. What is plain is that it was not inevitable ; it was not, as was said, the only possible course ; there were plenty of other courses ; there were plenty of other colours in the box. Again, in the discussion about Socialism, it is repeatedly rubbed into the public mind that we must choose between Socialism and some horrible thing that they call Individualism. I don't know what it means, but it seems to mean that anybody who happens to pull out a plum is to adopt the moral philosophy of the young Horner—and say what a good boy he is for helping himself. It is calmly assumed that the only two possible types of society are a Collectivist type of society and the type of society that exists at this moment and is rather like an animated muck-heap. It is quite unnecessary to say that I should prefer Socialism to the present state of things. I should prefer anarchism to the present state of things. But it is simply not the fact that Collectivism is the only other scheme for a more equal order. A Collectivist has a perfect right to think it the only sound scheme ; but it is not the only plausible or possible scheme. We might have peasant proprietorship ; we might have

the compromise of Henry George ; we might have a number of tiny communes ; we might have co-operation; we might have Anarchist Communism; we might have a hundred things. I am not saying that any of these are right, though I cannot imagine that any of them could be worse than the present social madhouse, with its top-heavy rich and its tortured poor ; but I say that it is an evidence of the stiff and narrow alternative offered to the civic mind, that the civic mind is not, generally speaking, conscious of these other possibilities. The civic mind is not free or alert enough to feel how much it has the world before it. There are at least ten solutions of the Education question, and no one knows which Englishmen really want. For Englishmen are only allowed to vote about the two which are at that moment offered by the Premier and the Leader of the Opposition. There are ten solutions of the drink question ; and no one knows which the democracy wants ; for the democracy is only allowed to light about one Licensing Bill at a time.

So that the situation comes to this : The democracy has a right to answer questions, but it has no right to ask them. It is still the political aristocracy that asks the questions.

44

The Voter and the Two Voices

And we shall not be unreasonably cynical if we suppose that the political aristocracy will always be rather careful what questions it asks. And if the dangerous comfort and self-flattery of modern England continues much longer there will be less democratic value in an English election than in a Roman saturnalia of slaves. For the powerful class will choose two courses of action, both of them safe for itself, and then give the democracy the gratification of taking one course or the other. The lord will take two things so much alike that he would not mind choosing from them blindfold —and then for a great jest he will allow the slaves to choose.

The Mad Official

OING mad is the slowest and dullest V_T business in the world. I have very nearly done it more than once in my boyhood, and so have nearly all my friends, born under the general doom of mortals, but especially of moderns ; I mean the doom that makes a man come almost to the end of thinking before he comes to the first chance of living.

But the process of going mad is dull, for the simple reason that a man does not know that it is going on. Routine and literalism and a certain dry-throated earnestness and mental thirst, these are the very atmosphere of morbidity. If once the man could become conscious of his madness, he would cease to be man. He studies certain texts in Daniel or cryptograms in Shakespeare through monstrously magnifying spectacles, which are on his nose night and day. If once he could take off the spectacles he would smash them. He deduces all his fantasies about the Sixth Seal or the Anglo-Saxon Race from one un-46

The Mad Official

examined and invisible first principle. If he could once see the first principle, he would see that it is not there.

This slow and awful self-hypnotism of error is a process that can occur not only with individuals, but also with whole societies. It is hard to pick out and prove ; that is why it is hard to cure. But this mental degeneration may be brought to one test, which I truly believe to be a real test. A nation is not going mad when it does extravagant things, so long as it does them in an extravagant spirit. Crusaders not cutting their beards till they found Jerusalem, Jacobins calling each other Harmodius and Epaminondas when their names were Jacques and Jules : these are wild things, but they were done in wild spirits at a wild moment.

But whenever we see things done wildly, but taken tamely, then the State is growing insane. For instance, I have a gun licence. For all I know, this would logically allow me to fire off fifty-nine enormous field-guns day and night in my back garden. I should not be surprised at a man doing it; for it would be great fun. But I should be surprised at the 47

A Miscellany of Men

neighbours putting up with it, and regarding it as an ordinary thing merely because it might happen to fulfil the letter of my licence. Or, again, I have a dog licence ; and I may have the right (for all I know) to turn ten thousand wild dogs loose in Buckinghamshire. I should not be surprised if the law were like that; because in modern England there is practically no law to be surprised at. I should not be . surprised even at the man who did it ; for a certain kind of man, if he lived long under the English landlord system, might do anything. But I should be surprised at the people who consented to stand it. I should, in other words, think the world a little mad if the incident were received in silence.

Now things every bit as wild as this are being received in silence every day. All strokes slip on the smoothness of a polished wall. All blows fall soundless on the softness of a padded cell. For madness is a passive as well as an active state : it is a paralysis, a refusal of the nerves to respond to the normal stimuli, as well as an unnatural stimulation. There are commonwealths, plainly to be 48

distinguished here and there in history, which pass from prosperity to squalor, or from glory to insignificance, or from freedom to slavery, not only in silence, but with serenity. The face still smiles while the limbs, literally and loathsomely, are dropping from the body. These are peoples that have lost the power of astonishment at their own actions. When they give birth to a fantastic fashion or a foolish law, they do not start or stare at the monster they have brought forth. They have grown used to their own unreason ; chaos is their cosmos ; and the whirlwind is the breath of their nostrils. These nations are really in danger of going off their heads en masse ; of becoming one vast vision of imbecility, with toppling cities and crazy country-sides, all dotted with industrious lunatics. One of these countries is modern England.

Now here is an actual, case of how our social cor tame in spirit, wild in tion ; a thing without I take this paragraph

"At Epping, bourne, a Lambournl 4
from

A Miscellany of Men

were summoned for neglecting their five children. Dr. Alpin said he was invited by the inspector of the N.S.P.C.C. to visit defendants' cottage. Both the cottage and the children were dirty. The children looked exceedingly well in health, but the conditions would be serious in case of illness. Defendants were stated to be sober. The man was discharged. The woman, who said she was hampered by the cottage having no water supply and that she was ill, was sentenced to six weeks' imprisonment. The sentence caused surprise, and the woman was removed crying, ' Lord, save me ! '

I know no name for this but Chinese. It calls up the mental picture of some archaic and changeless Eastern Court, in which men with dried faces and stiff ceremonial costumes perform some atrocious cruelty to the accompaniment of formal proverbs and sentences of which the very meaning has been forgotten. In both cases the only thing in the whole farrago that can be called real is the wrong. If we apply the lightest touch of reason to the whole Epping prosecution it dissolves into nothing.

I here challenge any person in his five wits to tell me what that woman was sent to prison 50

for. Either it was for being poor, or it was for being ill. Nobody could suggest, nobody will suggest, nobody, as a matter of fact, did suggest, that she had committed any other crime. The doctor was called in by a Society for the Prevention of Cruelty to Children. Was this woman guilty of cruelty to children ? Not in the least. Did the doctor say she was guilty of cruelty to children ? Not in the least. Was there any evidence even remotely bearing on the sin of cruelty ? Not a rap. The worst that the doctor could work himself up to saying was that though the children were " exceedingly " well, the conditions would be serious in case of illness. If the doctor will tell me any conditions that would be comic in case of illness, I shall attach more weight to his argument.

Now this is the worst effect of modern worry. The mad doctor has gone mad. He is literally and practically mad ; and still he is quite literally and practically a doctor. The only question is the old one, Quis docebit ipsum doctor em ? Now cruelty to children is an utterly unnatural thing; instinctively accursed of earth and heaven. But neglect of children is a natural thing ; like neglect of any other duty. It is a mere difference of

degree that divides extending arms and legs in calisthenics and extending them on the rack. It is a mere difference of degree that separates any operation from any torture. The thumb-screw can easily be called Manicure. Being pulled about by wild horses can easily be called Massage. The modern problem is not so much what people will endure as what they will not endure. But I fear I interrupt. . . . The boiling oil is boiling; and the Tenth Mandarin is already reciting the " Seventeen Serious Principles and the Fifty-three Virtues of the Sacred Emperor."

The Enchanted Man

WHEN I arrived to see the performance of the Buckinghamshire Players, who acted Miss Gertrude Robins's Pot Luck at Naphill a short time ago, it is the distressing, if scarcely surprising, truth that I entered very late. This would have mattered little, I hope, to any one, but that late comers had to be forced into front seats. For a real popular English audience always insists on crowding in the back part of the hall; and (as I have found in many an election) will endure the most unendurable taunts rather than come forward. The English are a modest people ; that is why they are entirely ruled and run by the few of them that happen to be immodest. In theatrical affairs the fact is strangely notable ; and in most playhouses we find the bored people in front and the eager people behind.

As far as the performance went I was quite the reverse of a bored person ; but I may have been a boring person, especially as I was thus S3

required to sit in the seats of the scornful. It will be a happy day in the dramatic world when all ladies have to take off their hats and all critics have to take off their heads. The people behind v-ill have a chance then. And as it happens, in this case, I had not so much taken off my head as lost it. I had lost it on the road ; on that strange journey that was the cause of my coming in late. I have a troubled recollection of having seen a very good play and made a very bad speech ; I have a cloudy recollection of talking to all sorts of nice people afterwards, but talking to them jerkily and with half a head, as a man talks when he has one eye on a clock.

And the truth is that I had one eye on an ancient and timeless clock, hung uselessly in heaven; whose very name has passed into a figure for such bemused folly. In the true sense of an ancient phrase, I was moonstruck. A lunar landscape, a scene of winter moonlight, had inexplicably got in between me and all other scenes. If any one had asked me I could not have said what it was ; I cannot say now. Nothing had occurred to me; except the breakdown of a hired motor on the ridge of a hill. It was not an adventure ; it was a vision.

The Enchanted Man

I had started in wintry twilight from my own door ; and hired a small car that found its way across the hills towards Naphill. But as night blackened and frost brightened and hardened it I found the way increasingly difficult; especially as the way was an incessant ascent. Whenever we topped a road like a staircase it was only to turn into a yet steeper road like a ladder.

At last, when I began to fancy that I was spirally climbing the Tower of Babel in a dream, I was brought to fact by alarming noises, stoppage, and the driver saying that " it couldn't be done." I got out of the car and suddenly forgot that I had ever been in it.

From the edge of that abrupt steep I saw something indescribable, which I am now going to describe. When Mr. Joseph Chamberlain delivered his great patriotic speech on the inferiority of England to the Dutch parts of South Africa, he made use of the expression " the illimitable veldt." The word " veldt " is Dutch, and the word " illimitable " is Double Dutch. But the meditative statesman probably meant that the new plains gave him a sense of largeness and dreariness which he had never found in England. Well, if he never found it in England it was because he never 55

looked for it in England. In England there is an illimitable number of illimitable veldts. I saw six or seven separate eternities in cresting as many different hills. One cannot find anything more infinite than a finite horizon, free and lonely and innocent. The Dutch veldt may be a little more desolate than Birmingham. But I am sure it is not so desolate as that English hill was, almost within a cannon-shot of High Wycombe.

I looked across a vast and voiceless valley straight at the moon, as if at a round mirror. It may have been the blue moon of the proverb ; for on that freezing night the very moon seemed blue with cold. A deathly frost fastened every branch and blade to its place. The sinking and softening forests, powdered with a grey frost, fell away underneath me into an abyss which seemed unfathomable. One fancied the world was soundless only because it was bottomless : it seemed as if all songs and cries had been swallowed in some unresisting stillness under the roots of the hills. I could fancy that if I shouted there would be no echo ; that if I hurled huge stones there would be no noise of reply. A dumb 56

devil had bewitched the landscape : but that again does not express the best or worst of it. All those hoary and frosted forests expressed something so unhuman that it has no human name. A horror of unconsciousness lay on them ; that is the nearest phrase I know. It was as if one were looking at the back of the world ; and the world did not know it. I had taken the universe in the rear. I was behind the scenes. I was eavesdropping upon an unconscious creation.

I shall not express what the place expressed. I am not even sure that it is a thing that ought to be expressed. There was something heathen about its union of beauty and death ; sorrow seemed to glitter, as it does in some of the great pagan poems. I understood one of the thousand poetical phrases of the populace, " a God-forsaken place." Yet something was present there ; and I could not yet find the key to my fixed impression. Then suddenly I remembered the right word. It was an enchanted place. It had been put to sleep. In a flash I remembered all the fairy-tales about princes turned to marble and princesses changed to snow. We were in a land where none could strive or cry out; a white nightmare. The moon looked at me across the 57

valley like the enormous eye of a hypnotist; the one white eve of the world.

There was never a better play than Pot Luck ; for it tells a tale with a point, and it is a tale that might happen any day among English peasants. There were never better actors than the local Buckinghamshire Players : for they were acting their own life with just that rise into exaggeration which is the transition from life to art. But all the time I was mesmerized by the moon; I saw all these men and women as enchanted things. The poacher shot pheasants ; the policeman tracked pheasants; the wife hid pheasants; they were all (especially the policeman) as true as death. But there was something more true to death than true to life about it all: the figures were frozen with a magic frost of sleep or fear or custom such as does not cramp the movements of the poor men of other lands. I looked at the poacher and the policeman and the gun ; then at the gun and the policeman and the poacher ; arid I could find no name for the fancy that haunted and escaped me. The poacher believed in the Game Laws as much as the policeman. The

The Enchanted Man

not only believed in the Game Laws, but protected them as well as him. She got a promise from her husband that he would never shoot another pheasant. Whether he kept it I doubt; I fancy he sometimes shot a pheasant even after that. But I am sure he never shot a policeman. For we live in an enchanted land.

The Sun Worshipper ^ ^> -o ^

THERE is a shrewd warning to be given to all people who are in revolt. And in the present state of things, I think all men are revolting in that sense ; except a few who are revolting in the other sense. But the warning to Socialists and other revolutionaries is this ; that as sure as fate, if they use any argument which is atheist or materialistic, that argument will always be turned against them at last by the tyrant and the slave. Today I saw one too common Socialist argument turned Tory, so to speak, in a manner quite startling and insane. I mean that modern doctrine, taught, I believe, by most followers of Karl Marx, which is called the materialist theory of history. The theory is, roughly, this : that all the important things in history are rooted in an economic motive. In short, history is a science ; a science of the search for food.

Now I desire, in passing only, to point out that this is not merely untrue, but actually 60

The Sun Worshipper

the reverse of the truth. It is putting it too feebly to say that the history of man is not only economic. Man would not have any history if he were only economic. The need for food is certainly universal, so universal that it is not even human. Cows have an economic motive, and apparently (I dare not say what ethereal delicacies may be in a cow) only an economic motive. The cow eats grass anywhere and never eats anything else. In short, the cow does fulfil the materialist theory of history : that is why the cow has no history. " A History of Cows " would be one of the simplest and briefest of standard works. But if some cows thought it wicked to eat long grass and persecuted all who did so ; if the cow with the crumpled horn were worshipped by some cows and gored to death by others ; if cows began to have obvious moral preferences over and above a desire for grass, then cows would begin to have a history. They would also begin to have a highly unpleasant time, which is perhaps the same thing.

The economic motive is not merely not inside all history ; it is actually outside all history. It belongs to Biology or the Science of Life ; 61

A Miscellany of Men

that is, it concerns things like cows, that are not so very much alive. Men are far too much alive to get into the science of anything ; for them we have made the art of history. To say that human actions have depended on economic support is like saying that they have depended on having two legs. It accounts for action, but not for such varied action ; it is a condition, but not a motive ; it is too universal to be useful. Certainly a soldier wins the Victoria Cross on two legs ; he also runs away on two legs. But if our object is to discover whether he will become a V.C. or a coward the most careful inspection of his legs will yield us little or no information. In the same way a man will want food if he is a dreamy romantic tramp, and will want food if he is a toiling and sweating millionaire. A man must be supported on food as he must be supported on legs. But cows (who have no history) are not only furnished more generously in the matter of legs, but can see their food on a much grander and more imaginative scale. A cow can lift up her eyes to the hills and see uplands and peaks of pure food. Yet we never see the horizon broken by crags of cake or happy mountains of cheese.

So far the cow (who has no history) seems to 62

have every other advantage. But history— the whole point of history—precisely is that some two-legged soldiers ran away while others, of similar anatomical structure, did not. The whole point of history precisely is : some people (like poets and tramps) chance getting money by disregarding it, while others (such as millionaires) will absolutely lose money for the fun of bothering about it. There would be no history if there were only economic history. All the historical events have been due to the twists and turns given to the economic instinct by forces that were not economic. For instance, this theory traces the French war of Edward III to a quarrel about the French wines. Any one who has even smelt the Middle Ages must feel fifty answers spring to his lips ; but in this case one will suffice. There would have been no such war, then, if we all drank water like cows. But when one is a man one enters the world of historic choice. The act of drinking wine is one that requires explanation. So is the act of not drinking wine.

But the capitalist can get much more fun out of the doctrine.

When strikes were splitting England right and left a little while ago, an ingenious writer, humorously describing himself as a Liberal, said that they were entirely due to the hot weather. The suggestion was eagerly taken up by other creatures of the same kind, and I really do not see why it was not carried farther and applied to other lamentable uprisings in history.

Thus, it is a remarkable fact that the weather is generally rather warm in Egypt; and this cannot but throw a light on the sudden and mysterious impulse of the Israelites to escape from captivity. The English strikers used some barren republican formula (arid as the definitions of the mediaeval schoolmen), some academic shibboleth about being free men and not being forced to work except for a wage accepted by them. Just in the same way the Israelites in Egypt employed some dry scholastic quibble about the extreme difficulty of making bricks with nothing to make them of. But whatever fantastic intellectual excuses they may have put forward for their strange and unnatural conduct in walking out when the prison door was open, there can be no doubt that the real cause was the warm weather. Such a climate 64

notoriously also produces delusions and horrible fancies, such as Mr. Kipling describes. And it was while their brains were disordered by the heat that the Jews fancied that they were founding a nation, that they were led by a prophet, and, in short, that they were going to be of some importance in the affairs of the world.

Nor can the historical student fail to note that the French monarchy was pulled down in August; and that August is a month in summer.

In spite of all this, however, I have some little difficulty myself in accepting so simple a form of the Materialist Theory of History (at these words all Marxian Socialists will please bow their heads three times), and I rather think that exceptions might be found to the principle. Yet it is not chiefly such exceptions that embarrass my belief in it.

No ; my difficulty is rather in accounting for the strange coincidence by which the shafts of Apollo split us exclusively along certain lines of class and of economics. I cannot understand why all solicitors did not leave off soliciting, all doctors leave off doctoring, all 5 65

judges leave off judging, all benevolent bankers leave off lending money at high interest, and all rising politicians leave off having nothing to add to what their right honourable friend told the House about eight years ago. The quaint theoretic plea of the workers, that they were striking because they were ill paid, seems to receive a sort of wild and hazy confirmation from the fact that, throughout the hottest weather, judges and other persons who are particularly well paid showed no disposition to strike. I have to fall back therefore on metaphysical fancies of my own ; and I continue to believe that the anger of the English poor (to steal a phrase from Sir Thomas Browne) came from something in man that is other than the elements and that owes no homage unto the sun.

When comfortable people come to talking stuff of that sort, it is really time that the comfortable classes made a short summary and confession of what they have really done with the very poor Englishman. The dawn of the mediaeval civilization found him a serf ; which is a different thing from a slave. He had security ; although the man belonged to 66

the land rather than the land to the man. He could not be evicted ; his rent could not be raised. In practice, it came to something like this : that if the lord rode down his cabbages he had not much chance of redress ; but he had the chance of growing more cabbages. He had direct access to the means of production.

Since then the centuries in England have achieved something different; and something which, fortunately, is perfectly easy to state. There is no doubt about what we have done. We have kept the inequality, but we have destroyed the security. The man is not tied to the land, as in serfdom; nor is the land tied to the man, as in a peasantry. The rich man has entered into an absolute ownership of farms and fields ; and (in the modern industrial phrase) he has locked out the English people. They can only find an acre to dig or a house to sleep in by accepting such competitive and cruel terms as he chooses to impose.

Well, what would happen then, over the larger parts of the planet, parts inhabited by savages ? Savages, of course, would hunt and fish. That retreat for the English poor was perceived ; and that retreat was cut off. 67

Game laws were made to extend over districts like the Arctic snows or the Sahara. The rich man had property over animals he had no more dreamed of than a governor of Roman Africa had dreamed of a giraffe. He owned all the birds that passed over his land : he might as well have owned all the clouds that passed over it. If a rabbit ran from Smith's land to Brown's land, it belonged to Brown, as if it were his pet dog. The logical answer to this would be simple: Any one stung on Brown's land ought to be able to prosecute Brown for keeping a dangerous wasp without a muzzle.

Thus the poor man was forced to be a tramp along the roads and to sleep in the open. That retreat was perceived ; and that retreat was cut off. A landless man in England can be punished for behaving in the only way that a landless man can behave : for sleeping under a hedge in Surrey or on a seat on the Embankment. His sin is described (with a hideous sense of fun) as that of having no visible means of subsistence.

The last possibility, of course, is that upon which all human beings would fall back if

they were sinking in a swamp or impaled on a spike or deserted on an island. It is that of calling out for pity to the passer-by. That retreat was perceived and that retreat was cut off. A man in England can be sent to prison for asking another man for help in the name of God.

You have done all these things, and by so doing you have forced the poor to serve the rich, and to serve them on the terms of the rich. They have still one weapon left against the extremes of insult and unfairness : that weapon is their numbers and the necessity of those numbers to the working of that vast and slavish machine. And because they still had this last retreat (which we call the Strike), because this retreat was also perceived, there was talk of this retreat being also cut off. Whereupon the workmen became suddenly and violently angry; and struck at your Boards and Committees here, there, and wherever they could. And you opened on them the eyes of owls, and said, " It must be the sunshine." You could only go on saying, " The sun, the sun." That was what the man in Ibsen said, when he had lost his wits.

The Wrong Incendiary ^> ^> *^> <^x

I STOOD looking at the Coronation Procession-—I mean the one in Beaconsfield ; not the rather elephantine imitation of it which, I believe, had some success in London •—and I was seriously impressed. Most of my life is passed in discovering Avith a deathly surprise that I was quite right. Never before have I realized how right I was in maintaining that the small area expresses the real patriotism : the smaller the field the taller the tower. There were things in our local procession that did not (one might even reverently say, could not) occur in the London procession. One of the most prominent citizens in our procession (for instance) had his face blacked. Another rode on a pony which wore pink and blue trousers. I was not present at the Metropolitan affair, and therefore my assertion is subject to such correction as the eye-witness may always offer to the absentee. But I believe with some firmness that no such features occurred in the London pageant. 70

The Wrong Incendiary

But it is not of the local celebration that I would speak, but of something that occurred before it. In the field beyond the end of my garden the materials for a bonfire had been heaped ; a hill of every kind of rubbish and refuse and things that nobody wants ; broken chairs, dead trees, rags, shavings, newspapers, new religions, in pamphlet form, reports of the Eugenic Congress, and so on. All this refuse, material and mental, it was our purpose to purify and change to holy flame on the day when the King was crowned. The following is an account of the rather strange thing that really happened. I do not know whether it was any sort of symbol; but I narrate it just as it befell.

In the middle of the night I woke up slowly and listened to what I supposed to be the heavy crunching of a cart-wheel along a road of loose stones. Then it grew louder, and I thought somebody was shooting out cartloads of stones ; then it seemed as if the shock was breaking big stones into pieces. Then I realized that under this sound there was also a strange, sleepy, almost inaudible roar ; and that on top of it every now and then came pigmy pops like a battle of penny pistols. Then I knew what it was. I went to the win-

A Miscellany of Men

dow ; and a great firelight flung across two meadows smote me where I stood. " Oh, my holy aunt," I thought, " they've mistaken the Coronation Day."

And yet when I eyed the transfigured scene it did not seem exactly like a bonfire or any ritual illumination. It was too chaotic, and too close to the houses of the town. All one side of a cottage was painted pink with the giant brush of flame ; the next side, by contrast, was painted as black as tar. Along the front of this ran a blackening rim or rampart edged with a restless red ribbon that danced and doubled and devoured like a scarlet snake ; and beyond it was nothing but a deathly fullness of light.

I put on some clothes and went down the road ; all the dull or startling noises in that din of burning growing louder and louder as I walked. The heaviest sound was that of an incessant cracking and crunching, as if some giant with teeth of stone was breaking up the bones of the world. I had not yet come within sight of the real heart and habitat of the fire ; but the strong red light, like an unnatural midnight sunset, powdered the greyest grass with gold and flushed the few tall trees up to the last fingers of their foliage. Behind 72

them the night was black and cavernous; and one could only trace faintly the ashen horizon beyond the dark and magic Wilton woods. As I went, a workman on a bicycle shot a rood past me ; then staggered from his machine and shouted to me to tell him where the fire was. I answered that I was going to see, but thought it was the cottages by the wood-yard. He said, "My God!" and vanished.

A little farther on I found grass and pavement soaking and flooded, and the red and yellow flames repainted in pools and puddles. Beyond were dim huddles of people and a small distant voice shouting out orders. The fire-engines were at work. I went on among the red reflections, which seemed like subterranean fires ; I had a singular sensation of being in a very important dream. Oddly enough, this was increased when I found that most of my friends and neighbours were entangled in the crowd. Only in dreams do we see familiar faces so vividly against a black background of midnight. I was glad to find (for the workman cyclist's sake) that the fire was not in the houses by the wood-yard, but in the wood-yard itself. There was no fear for human life, and the thing was

seemingly accidental, though there were the usual ugly whispers about rivalry and revenge. But for all that I could not shake off my dream-drugged soul a swollen, tragic, portentous sort of sensation, that it all had something to do with the crowning of the English King, and the glory or the end of England. It was not till I saw the puddles and the ashes in broad daylight next morning that I was fundamentally certain that my midnight adventure had not happened outside this world.

But I was more arrogant than the ancient Emperors Pharaoh or Nebuchadnezzar ; for I attempted to interpret my own dream. The fire was feeding upon solid stacks of unused beech or pine, grey and white piles of virgin wood. It was an orgy of mere waste ; thousands of good things were being killed before they had ever existed. Doors, tables, walking-sticks, wheelbarrows, wooden swords for boys, Dutch dolls for girls-— I could hear the cry of each uncreated thing as it expired in the flames. And then I thought of that other noble tower of needless things that stood in the field beyond my garden ; the bonfire, the mountain of vanities, that is meant for burning ; and how it stood dark and lonely in the 74

meadow, and the birds hopped on its corners and the dew touched and spangled its twigs. And I remembered that there are two kinds of fires, the Bad Fire and the Good Fire— the last must surely be the meaning of Bonfire. And the paradox is that the Good Fire is made of bad things, of things that we do not want ; but the Bad Fire is made of good things, of things that we do want; like all that wealth of wood that might have made dolls and chairs and tables, but was only making a hueless ash.

And then I saw, in my vision, that just as there are two fires, so there are two revolutions. And I saw that the whole mad modern world is a race between them. Which will happen first — the revolution in which bad things shall perish, or that other revolution, in which good things shall perish also ? One is the riot that all good men, even the most conservative, really dream of, when the sneer shall be struck from the face of the well-fed ; when the wine of honour shall be poured down the throat of despair ; when we shall, so far as to the sons of flesh is possible, take tyranny and usury and public treason and bind them into bundles and burn them. And the other is the disruption that may come 75 prematurely, negatively, and suddenly in the night; like the fire in my little town.

It may come because the mere strain of modern life is unbearable ; and in it even the things that men do desire may break down : marriage and fair ownership and worship and the mysterious worth of man. The two revolutions, white and black, are racing each other like two railway trains ; I cannot guess the issue . . . but even as I thought of it, the tallest turret of the timber stooped and faltered and came down in a cataract of noises. And the fire, finding passage, went up with a spout like a fountain. It stood far up among the stars for an instant, a blazing pillar of brass fit for a pagan conqueror, so high that one could fancy it visible away among the goblin trees of Burnham or along the terraces of the Chiltern Hills.

The Free Man

THE idea of liberty has ultimately a religious root; that is why men find it so easy to die for and so difficult to define. It refers finally to the fact that, while the oyster and the palm tree have to save their lives by law, man has to save his soul by choice. Ruskin rebuked Coleridge for praising freedom, and said that no man would wish the sun to be free. It seems enough to answer that no man would wish to be the sun. Speaking as a Liberal, I have much more sympathy with the idea of Joshua stopping the sun in heaven than with the idea of Ruskin trotting his daily round in imitation of its regularity. Joshua was a Radical, and his astronomical act was distinctly revolutionary. For all revolution is the mastering of matter by the spirit of man, the emergence of that human authority within us which, in the noble words of Sir Thomas Browne, " owes no homage unto the sun."

A Miscellany of Men

Generally, the moral substance of liberty is this : that man is not meant merely to receive good laws, good food, or good conditions, like a tree in a garden, but is meant to take a certain princely pleasure in selecting and shaping, like the gardener. Perhaps that is the meaning of the trade of Adam. And the best popular words for rendering the real idea of liberty are those which speak of man as a creator. We use the word " make" about most of the things in which freedom is essential, as a country walk or a friendship or a love affair. When a man " makes his way " through a wood, he has really created : he has built a road, like the Romans. When a man " makes a friend " he makes a man. And in the third case we talk of a man " making love," as if he were (as indeed he is) creating new masses and colours of that flaming material— an awful form of manufacture.

In its primary spiritual sense, liberty is the god in man, or, if you like the word, the artist. In its secondary political sense liberty is the living influence of the citizen on the State in the direction of moulding or deflecting it. Men are the only creatures that evidently possess it. On the one hand, the eagle has no liberty ; he only has loneliness. On the other 78

The Free Man

hand, ants, bees, and beavers exhibit the highest miracle of the State influencing the citizen, but no perceptible trace of the citizen influencing the State. You may, if you like, call the ants a democracy as you may call the bees a despotism. But I fancy that the architectural ant who attempted to introduce an art nouveau style of ant-hill would have a career as curt and fruitless as the celebrated bee who wanted to swarm alone. The isolation of this idea in humanity is akin to its religious character; but it is not even in humanity by any means equally distributed. The idea that the State should not only be supported by its children, like the ant-hill, but should be constantly criticized and reconstructed by them, is an idea stronger in Christendom than any other part of the planet; stronger in Western than Eastern Europe. And touching the pure idea of the individual being free to speak and act within limits, the assertion of this idea, we may fairly say, has been the peculiar honour of our own country. For my part I greatly prefer the Jingoism of Rule Britannia to the Imperialism of The Recessional. I have no objection to Britannia ruling the waves. I draw the line when she begins to rule the dry land——and such damn-79

ably dry land toe*—as in Africa. And there was a real old English sincerity in the vulgar chorus that " Britons never shall be slaves." We had no equality and hardly any justice ; but freedom we were really fond of. And I think just now it is worth while to draw attention to the old optimistic prophecy that " Britons never shall be slaves."

The mere love of liberty has never been at a lower ebb in England than it has been for the last twenty years. Never before has it been so easy to slip small Bills through Parliament for the purpose of locking people up. Never was it so easy to silence awkward questions, or to protect high-placed officials. Two hundred years ago we turned out the Stuarts rather than endanger the Habeas Corpus Act. Quite recently we abolished the Habeas Corpus Act rather than turn out the Home Secretary. We passed a law (which is now in force) that an Englishman's punishment shall not depend upon judge and jury, but upon the governors and jailers who have got hold of him. But this is not the only case. The scorn of liberty is in the air. A newspaper is seized by the police in Trafalgar Square 80

without a word of accusation or explanation. The Home Secretary says that in his opinion the police are very nice people, and there is an end of the matter. A Member of Parliament attempts to criticize a peerage. The Speaker says he must not criticize a peerage, and there the matter drops.

Political liberty, let us repeat, consists in the power of criticizing those flexible parts of the State which constantly require reconsideration, not the basis, but the machinery. In plainer words, it means the power of saying the sort of things that a decent but discontented citizen wants to say. He does not want to spit on the Bible, or to run about without clothes, or to read the worst page in Zola from the pulpit of St. Paul's. Therefore the forbidding of these things (whether just or not) is only tyranny in a secondary and special sense. It restrains the abnormal, not the normal man. But the normal man, the decent discontented citizen, does want to protest against unfair law courts. He does want to expose brutalities of the police. He does want to make game of a vulgar pawnbroker who is made a Peer. He does want publicly to warn people against unscrupulous capitalists and suspicious finance. If he is run in 6 81

for doing this (as he will be) he does want to proclaim the character or known prejudices of the magistrate who tries him. If he is sent to prison (as he will be) he does want to have a clear and civilized sentence, telling him when he will come out. And these are literally and exactly the things that he now cannot get. That is the almost cloying humour of the present situation. I can say abnormal things in modern magazines. It is the normal things that I am not allowed to say. I can write in some solemn quarterly an elaborate article explaining that God is the devil; I can write in some cultured weekly an aesthetic fancy describing how I should like to eat boiled baby. The thing I must not write is rational criticism of the men and institutions of my country.

The present condition of England is briefly this : That no Englishman can say in public a twentieth part of what he says in private. One cannot say, for instance, that'—•— But I am afraid I must leave out that instance, because one cannot say it. I cannot prove my case——because it is so true.

The Hypothetical Householder

WE have read of some celebrated philosopher who was so absent-minded that he paid a call at his own house. My own absent-mindedness is extreme, and my philosophy, of course, is the marvel of men and angels. But I never quite managed to be so absent-minded as that. Some yards at least from my own door something vaguely familiar has always caught my eye ; and thus the joke has been spoiled. Of course I have quite constantly walked into another man's house, thinking it was my own house ; my visits became almost monotonous. But walking into my own house and thinking it was another man's house is a flight of poetic detachment still beyond me. Something of the sensations that such an absent-minded man must feel I really felt the other day ; and very pleasant sensations they were. The best parts of every proper romance are the first chapter and the last chapter ; and to knock at a strange door and find a nice wife 83

would be to concentrate the beginning and end of all romance.

Mine was a milder and slighter experience, but its thrill was of the same kind. For I strolled through a place I had imagined quite virgin and unvisited (as far as I was concerned), and I suddenly found I was treading in my own footprints, and the footprints were nearly twenty years old.

; It was one of those stretches of country which always suggest an almost unnatural decay; thickets and heaths that have grown out of what were once great gardens. Garden flowers still grow there as wild flow r ers, as it says in some good poetic couplet which I forget ; and there is something singularly romantic and disastrous about seeing things that were so long a human property and care fighting for their own hand in the thicket. One almost expects to find a decayed dog-kennel ; with the dog evolved into a wolf.

This desolate garden-land had been even in my youth scrappily planned out for building. The half-built or empty houses had appeared quite threateningly on the edge of this heath even when I walked over it years 84

ago and almost as a boy. I was astonished that the building had gone no farther ; I suppose somebody went bankrupt and somebody else disliked building. But I remember, especially along one side of this tangle or coppice, that there had once been a row of half-built houses. The brick of which they were built was a sort of plain pink; everything else was a blinding white ; the houses smoked with white dust and white sawdust; and on many of the windows were rubbed those round rough disks of white which always delighted me as a child. They looked like the white eyes of some blind giant.

I could see the crude, parched, pink-and-white villas still, though I had not thought at all of them for a quarter of my life, and had not thought much of them even when I saw them. Then I was an idle, but eager youth walking out from London ; now I was a most reluctantly busy middle-aged person coming in from the country. Youth, I think, seems farther off than childhood, for it made itself more of a secret. Like a prenatal picture, distant, tiny, and quite distinct, I saw this heath on which I stood; and I looked around for the string of bright, half-baked villas. They still stood there; but 85

they were quite russet and weather-stained, as if they had stood for centuries.

I remembered exactly what I had done on that day long ago. I had half slid on a miry descent: it was still there ; a little lower I had knocked off the top of a thistle : the thistles had not been discouraged, but were still growing. I recalled it because I had wondered why one knocks off the tops of thistles ; and then I had thought of Tarquin ; and then I had recited most of Macaulay's Firginius to myself, for I was young. And then I came to a tattered edge where the very tuft had whitened with the sawdust and brick-dust from the new row of houses ; and two or three green stars of dock and thistle grew spasmodically about the blinding road.

I remembered how I had walked up this new one-sided street all those years ago ; and I remembered what I had thought. I thought that this red and white glaring terrace at noon was really more creepy and more lonesome than a glimmering churchyard at midnight. The churchyard could only be full of the ghosts of the dead ; but these houses were full of the ghosts of the unborn. And a man 86

The Hypothetical Householder

can never find a home in the future as he can find it in the past. I was always fascinated by that medieval notion of erecting a rudely carpentered stage in the street, and acting on it a miracle play of the Holy Family or the Last Judgment. And I thought to myself that each of these glaring, gaping, new jerry-built boxes was indeed a rickety stage erected for the acting of a real miracle play ; of that human family that is almost the holy one, and of that human death that is near to the last judgment.

For some foolish reason the last house but one in that imperfect row especially haunted me with its hollow grin and empty window-eyes. Something in the shape of this brick-and-mortar skeleton was attractive ; and there being no workmen about, I strolled into it for curiosity and .solitude. I gave, with all the sky-deep gravity of youth, a benediction upon the man who was going to live there. I even remember that for the convenience of meditation I called him James Harrogate.

As I reflected it crawled back into my memory that I had mildly played the fool in that house on that distant day. I had some red chalk in my pocket, I think, and I wrote things on the unpapered plaster walls ; things 87

A Miscellany of Men

addressed to Mr. Harrogate. A dim memory told me that I had written up in what I supposed to be the dining-room :

James Harrogate, thank God for meat, Then eat and eat and eat and eat,

or something of that kind. I faintly feel that some longer lyric was scrawled on the walls of what looked like a bedroom, something beginning :

When laying what you call your head, O Harrogate, upon your bed,

and there all my memory dislimns and decays. But I could still see quite vividly the plain plastered walls and the rude, irregular writing, and the places where the red chalk broke. I could see them, I mean, in memory; for when I came down that road again after a sixth of a century the house was very different.

I had seen it before at noon, and now I found it in the dusk. But its windows glowed with lights of many artificial sorts ; one of its low square windows stood open ; from this there escaped up the road a stream of lamplight and a stream of singing. Some sort of girl, at least, was standing at some sort of piano, 88

The Hypothetical Householder

and singing a song of healthy sentimentalism in that house where long ago my blessing had died on the wind and my poems been covered up by the wallpaper. I stood outside that lamplit house at dusk full of those thoughts that I shall never express if I live to be a million any better than I expressed them in red chalk upon the wall. But after I had hovered a little, and was about to withdraw, a mad impulse seized me. I rang the bell. I said in distinct accents to a very smart suburban maid, " Does Mr. James Harrogate live here ? "

She said he didn't; but that she would inquire, in case I was looking for him in the neighbourhood ; but I excused her from such exertion. I had one moment's impulse to look for him all over the world ; and then decided not to look for him at all.

The Priest of Spring *^ ^> ^> ^>

THE sun has strengthened and the air softened just before Easter Day. But it is a troubled brightness which has a breath not only of novelty but of revolution. There are two great armies of the human intellect who will fight till the end on this vital point, whether Easter is to be congratulated on fitting in with the Spring—or the Spring on fitting in with Easter.

The only two things that can satisfy the soul arc a person and a story ; and even a story must be about a person. There are indeed very voluptuous appetites and enjoyments in mere abstractions'—like mathematics, logic, or chess. But these mere pleasures of the mind are like mere pleasures of the body. That is, they are mere pleasures, though they may be gigantic pleasures ; they can never by a mere increase of themselves amount to happiness. A man just about to be hanged may enjoy his breakfast, espe-90

cially if it be his favourite breakfast; and in the same way he may enjoy an argument with the chaplain about heresy, especially if it is his favourite heresy. But whether he can enjoy either of them does not depend on either of them ; it depends upon his spiritual attitude towards a subsequent event. And that event is really interesting to the soul; because it is the end of a story and (as some hold) the end of a person.

Now it is this simple truth which, like many others, is too simple for our scientists to see. This is where they go wrong, not only about true religion, but about false religions too ; so that their account of mythology is more mythical than the myth itself. I do not confine myself to saying that they are quite incorrect when they state (for instance) that Christ was a legend of dying and reviving vegetation, like Adonis or Persephone. I say that even if Adonis was a god of vegetation, they have got the whole notion of him wrong. Nobody, to begin with, is sufficiently interested in decaying vegetables, as such, to make any particular mystery or disguise about them ; and certainly 91

not enough to disguise them under the image of a very handsome young man, which is a vastly more interesting thing. If Adonis was connected with the fall of leaves in autumn and the return of flowers in spring, the process of thought was quite different. It is a process of thought which springs up spontaneously in all children and young artists ; it springs up spontaneously in all healthy societies. It is very difficult to explain in a diseased society.

The brain of man is subject to short and strange snatches of sleep. A cloud seals the city of reason or rests upon the sea of imagination ; a dream that darkens as much, whether it is a nightmare of atheism or a day-dream of idolatry. And just as we have all sprung from sleep with a start and found ourselves saying some sentence that has no meaning, save in the mad tongues of the midnight, so the human mind starts from its trances of stupidity with some complete phrase upon its lips : a complete phrase which is a complete folly. Unfortunately it is not like the dream sentence, generally forgotten in the putting on of boots or the putting in of breakfast. This senseless aphorism, invented when man's mind was asleep, still hangs on his tongue and 92 entangles all his relations to rational and daylight things. All our controversies are confused by certain kinds of phrases which are not merely untrue, but were always unmeaning ; which are not merely inapplicable, but were always intrinsically useless. We recognize them wherever a man talks of " the survival of the fittest," meaning only the survival of the survivors ; or wherever a man says that the rich " have a stake in the country," as if the poor could not suffer from misgovernment or military defeat; or where a man talks about " going on towards Progress," Avhich only means going on towards going on ; or when a man talks about " government by the wise few," as if they could be picked out by their pantaloons. " The wise few " must mean either the few whom the foolish think wise or the very foolish who think themselves wise.

There is one piece of nonsense that modern people still find themselves saying, even after they are more or less awake, by which I am particularly irritated. It arose in the popularized science of the nineteenth century, especially in connection with the study of myths and religions. The fragment of gibberish to which I refer generally takes the

form of saying " This god or hero really represents the sun." Or " Apollo killing the Python means that the summer drives out the winter." Or " The King dying in a western battle is a symbol of the sun setting in the west." Now I should really have thought that even the sceptical professors, whose skulls are as shallow as frying-pans, might have reflected that human beings never think or feel like this. Consider what is involved in this supposition. It presumes that primitive man went out for a walk and saw with great interest a big burning spot on the sky. He then said to primitive woman, " My dear, we had better keep this quiet. We mustn't let it get about. The children and the slaves are so very sharp. They might discover the sun any day, unless we are very careful. So we won't call it ' the sun,' but I will draw a picture of a man killing a snake ; and \vhenever I do that you will know what I mean. The sun doesn't look at all like a man killing a snake; so nobody can possibly know. It will be a little secret between us ; and while the slaves and the children fancy I am quite excited with a grand tale of a writhing dragon and a wrestling demigod, I shall really mean this delicious little discovery,

The Priest of Spring

that there is a round yellow disk up in the air." One does not need to know much mythology to know that this is a myth. It is commonly called the Solar Myth.

Quite plainly, of course, the case was just the other way. The god was never a symbol or hieroglyph representing the sun. The sun was a hieroglyph representing the god. Primitive man (with whom my friend Dombey is no doubt well acquainted) went out with his head full of gods and heroes, because that is the chief use of having a head. Then he saw the sun in some glorious crisis of the dominance of noon or the distress of nightfall, and he said, " That is how the face of the god would shine when he had slain the dragon," or " That is how the whole world would bleed to westward, if the god were slain at last."

No human being was ever really so unnatural as to worship Nature. No man, however indulgent (as I am) to corpulency, ever worshipped a man as round as the sun or a woman as round as the moon. No man, however attracted to an artistic attenuation, ever really believed that the Dryad was as lean and stiff as the tree. We human beings have never worshipped Nature ; and indeed, 95

the reason is very simple. It is that all human beings are superhuman beings. We have printed our own image upon Nature, as God has printed His image upon us. We have told the enormous sun to stand still; we have fixed him on our shields, caring no more for a star than for a starfish. And when there were powers of Nature we could not for the time control, we have conceived great beings in human shape controlling them. Jupiter does not mean thunder. Thunder means the march and victory of Jupiter. Neptune does not mean the sea ; the sea is his, and he made it. In other words, what the savage really said about the sea was, " Only my fetish Mumbo could raise such mountains out of mere water." What the savage really said about the sun was, " Only my great-greatgrandfather Jumbo could deserve such a blazing crown."

About all these myths my own position is utterly and even sadly simple. I say you cannot really understand any myths till you have found that one of them is not a myth. Turnip ghosts mean nothing if there are no real ghosts. Forged bank-notes mean nothing if there are no real bank-notes. Heathen gods mean nothing, and must always mean nothing, 96

to those of us that deny the Christian God. When once a god is admitted, even a false god, the Cosmos begins to know its place : which is the second place. When once it is the real God the Cosmos falls down before Him, offering flowers in spring as flames in winter. " My love is like a red, red rose " does not mean that the poet is praising roses under the allegory of a young lady. " My love is an arbutus " does not mean that the author was a botanist so pleased with a particular arbutus tree that he said he loved it. " Who art the moon and regent of my sky " does not mean that Juliet invented Romeo to account for the roundness of the moon. " Christ is the Sun of Easter " does not mean that the worshipper is praising the sun under the emblem of Christ. Goddess or god can clothe themselves with the spring or summer ; but the body is more than raiment. Religion takes almost disdainfully the dress of Nature ; and indeed Christianity has done as well with the snows of Christmas as with the snowdrops of spring. And when I look across the sun-struck fields, I know in my inmost bones that my joy is not solely in the spring: for spring alone, being always returning, would be always sad. There is somebody or some-7 97

thing walking there, to be crowned with flowers : and my pleasure is in some promise yet possible and in the resurrection of the dead.

98

The Real Journalist

OUR age which has boasted of realism will fail chiefly through lack of reality. Never, I fancy, has there been so grave and startling a divorce between the real way a thing is done and the look of it when it is done. I take the nearest and most topical instance to hand—a newspaper. Nothing looks more neat and regular than a newspaper, with its parallel columns, its mechanical printing, its detailed facts and figures, its responsible, polysyllabic leading articles. Nothing, as a matter of fact, goes every night through more agonies of adventure, more hairbreadth escapes, desperate expedients, crucial councils, random compromises, or barely averted catastrophes. Seen from the outside, it seems to come round as automatically as the clock and as silently as the dawn. Seen from the inside, it gives all its organizers a gasp of relief every morning to see that it has come out at all; that it has come out without the leading 99

A Miscellany of Men

article upside down or the Pope congratulated on discovering the North Pole.

I will give an instance (merely to illustrate my thesis of unreality) from the paper that I know best. Here is a simple story, a little episode in the life of a journalist, which may be amusing and instructive : the tale of how I made a great mistake in quotation. There are really two stories: the story as seen from the outside, by a man reading the paper ; and the story seen from the inside, by the journalists shouting and telephoning and taking notes in shorthand through the night.

This is the outside story ; and it reads like a dreadful quarrel. The notorious G. K. Chesterton, a reactionary Torquemada whose one gloomy pleasure was in the defence of orthodoxy and the pursuit of heretics, long calculated and at last launched a denunciation of a brilliant leader of the New Theology which he hated with all the furnace of his fanatic soul. In this document Chesterton darkly, deliberately, and not having the fear of God before his eyes, asserted that Shakespeare wrote the line " that wreathes its old fantastic

roots so high." This he said because he had been kept in ignorance by Priests; or, perhaps, because he thought craftily that none of his dupes could discover a curious and forgotten rhyme called Elegy in a Country Churchyard. Anyhow, that orthodox gentleman made a howling error ; and received some twenty - five letters and post - cards from kind correspondents who pointed out the mistake.

But the odd thing is that scarcely any of them could conceive that it was a mistake. The first wrote in the tone of one wearied of epigrams, and cried, " What is the joke now ? " Another professed (and practised, for all I know, God help him) that he had read through all Shakespeare and failed to find the line. A third wrote in a sort of moral distress, asking, as in confidence, if Gray was really a plagiarist. They were a noble collection ; but they all subtly assumed an element of leisure and exactitude in the recipient's profession and character which is far from the truth. Let us pass on to the next act of the external tragedy.

In Monday's issue of the same paper appeared a letter from the same culprit. He ingenuously confessed that the line did not belong to 101

Shakespeare, but to a poet whom he called Grey. Which was another cropper — or whopper. This strange and illiterate outbreak was printed by the editor with the justly scornful title, " Mr. Chesterton ' Explains ' ? " Any man reading the paper at breakfast saw at once the meaning of the sarcastic quotation marks. They meant, of course, " Here is a man who doesn't know Gray from Shakespeare ; he tries to patch it up and he can't even spell Gray. And that is what he calls an Explanation." That is the perfectly natural inference of the reader from the letter, the mistake, and the headline — as seen from the outside. The falsehood was serious ; the editorial rebuke was serious. The stern editor and the sombre, baffled contributor confront each other as the curtain falls.

And now I will tell you exactly what really happened. It is honestly rather amusing ; it is a story of what journals and journalists really are. A monstrously lazy man lives in South Bucks partly by writing a column in the Saturday Daily Neves. At the time he usually

writes it (which is always at the last moment) his house is unexpectedly invaded by infants of all shapes and sizes. His secretary is called away ; and he has to cope with the invading pigmies. Playing with children is a glorious thing ; but the journalist in question has never understood why it was considered a soothing or idyllic one. It reminds him, not of watering little budding flowers, but of wrestling for hours with gigantic angels and devils. Moral problems of the most monstrous complexity besiege him incessantly. He has to decide before the awful eyes of innocence, whether, when a sister has knocked down a brother's bricks, in revenge for the brother having taken two sweets out of his turn, it is endurable that the brother should retaliate by scribbling on the sister's picture-book, and whether such conduct does not justify the sister in blowing out the brother's unlawfully lighted match.

Just as he is solving this problem upon principles of the highest morality, it occurs to him suddenly that he has not written his Saturday article; and that there is only about an hour to do it in. He wildly calls to somebody (probably the gardener) to telephone to somewhere for a messenger ; he barricades 103

himself in another room and tears his hair, wondering what on earth he shall write about. A drumming of fists on the door outside and a cheerful bellowing encourage and clarify his thoughts ; and he is able to observe some newspapers and circulars in wrappers lying on the table. One is a dingy book catalogue ; the second is a shiny pamphlet about petrol; the third is a paper called The Christian Commonwealth. He opens it anyhow, and sees in the middle of a page a sentence with which he honestly disagrees. It says that the sense of beauty in Nature is a new thing, hardly felt before Wordsworth. A stream of images and pictures pour through his head, like skies chasing each other or forests running by. *' Not felt before Wordsworth ! " he thinks. *" Oh, but this won't do ... bare ruined choirs where late the sweet birds sang . . . night's candles are burnt out . . . glowed with living sapphires . . . leaving their moon-loved maze . . . antique roots fantastic . . . antique roots wreathed high . . . what is it in As You Like It?"

He sits doAvn desperately ; the messenger
rings at the bell; the children drum on the
door ; the servants run up from time to time
to say the messenger is getting bored ; and
104

The Real Journalist

the pencil staggers along, making the world a present of fifteen hundred unimportant words, and making Shakespeare a present of a portion of Gray's Elegy ; putting " fantastic roots \vreathed high " instead of " antique roots peep out." Then the journalist sends off his copy and turns his attention to the enigma of whether a brother should commandeer a sister's necklace because the sister pinched him at Littlehampton. That is the first scene; that is how an article is really written.

The scene now changes to the newspaper office. The writer of the article has discovered his mistake and wants to correct it by the next day : but the next day is Sunday. He cannot post a letter, so he rings up the paper and dictates a letter by telephone. He leaves the title to his friends at the other end ; he knows that they can spell " Gray," as no doubt they can : but the letter is put down by journalistic custom in a pencil scribble and the vowel may well be doubtful. The friend writes at the top of the letter " ' G. K. C.' Explains," putting the initials in quotation 105

marks. The next man passing it for press is bored with these initials (I am with him there) and crosses them out, substituting \vith austere civility, " Mr. Chesterton Explains." But-—and now we hear the iron laughter of the Fates, for the blind bolt is about to fall—— but he neglects to cross out the second " quote" (as we call it) and it goes up to press with a " quote " between the last words. Another quotation mark at the end of " explains " was the work of one merry moment for the printers upstairs. So the inverted commas were lifted entirely off one word on to the other and a totally innocent title suddenly turned into a blasting sneer. But that would have mattered nothing so far, for there was nothing to sneer at. In the same dark hour, however, there was a printer who was (I suppose) so devoted to this Government that he could think of no Gray but Sir Edward Grey. He spelt it " Grey " by a mere misprint, and the whole tale was complete : first blunder, second blunder, and final condemnation.

That is a little tale of journalism as it is ; if you call it egotistic and ask what is the 106
use of it I think I could tell you. You might remember it when next some ordinary young workman is going to be hanged by the neck on circumstantial evidence.

The Sentimental Scot ^> ^> ^> -Q>

OF all the great nations of Christendom, the Scotch are by far the most romantic. I have just enough Scotch experience and just enough Scotch blood to know this in the only way in which a thing can really be known ; that is, when the outer world and the inner world are at one. I know it is always said that the Scotch are practical, prosaic, and puritan ; that they have an eye to business.

I like that phrase " an eye " to business. Polyphemus had an eye for business ; it was in the middle of his forehead. It served him admirably for the only two duties which are demanded in a modern financier and captain of industry : the two duties of counting sheep and of eating men. But when that one eye was put out he was done for. But the Scotch are not one-eyed practical men, though their best friends must admit that they are occasionally business-like. They are, quite fundamentally, romantic and sentimental, and this 108

The Sentimental Scot

is proved by the very economic argument that is used to prove their harshness and hunger for the material. The mass of Scots have accepted the industrial civilization, with its factory chimneys and its famine prices, with its steam and smoke and steel— and strikes. The mass of the Irish have not accepted it. The mass of the Irish have clung to agriculture with claws of iron; and have succeeded in keeping it. That is because the Irish, though far inferior to the Scotch in art and literature, are hugely superior to them in practical politics. You do need to be very romantic to accept the industrial civilization. It does really require all the old Gaelic glamour to make men think that Glasgow is a grand place. Yet the miracle is achieved ; and while I was in Glasgow I shared the illusion. I have never had the faintest illusion about Leeds or Birmingham. The industrial dream suited the Scots. Here was a really romantic vista, suited to a romantic people; a vision of higher and higher chimneys taking hold upon the heavens, of fiercer and fiercer fires in which adamant could evaporate like dew. Here were taller and taller engines that began already to shriek and gesticulate like giants. Here were thunderbolts of communics 109

[L

which already flashed to and fro like thoughts. It was unreasonable to expect the rapt, dreamy, romantic Scot to stand still in such a whirl of wizardry to ask whether he, the ordinary Scot, would be any the richer.

He, the ordinary Scot, is very much the poorer. Glasgow is not a rich city. It is a particularly poor city ruled by a few particularly rich men. It is not, perhaps, quite so poor a city as Liverpool, London, Manchester, Birmingham, or Bolton. It is vastly poorer than Rome, Rouen, Munich, or Cologne. A certain civic vitality notable in Glasgow may, perhaps, be due to the fact that the high poetic patriotism of the Scots has there been reinforced by the cutting common sense and independence of the Irish. In any case, I think there can be no doubt of the main historical fact. The Scotch were tempted by the enormous but unequal opportunities of industrialism, because the Scotch are romantic. The Irish refused those enormous and unequal opportunities, because the Irish are clearsighted. They would not need very clear sight by this time to see that in England and Scot-

land the temptation has been a betrayal. The industrial system has failed.

I was coming the other day along a great valley road that strikes out of the westland counties about Glasgow, more or less towards the east and the widening of the Forth. It may, for all I know (I amused myself with the fancy), be the way along which Wallace came with his crude army, when he gave battle before Stirling Brig ; and, in the midst of medieval diplomacies, made a new nation possible. Anyhow, the romantic quality of Scotland rolled all about me, as much in the last reek of Glasgow as in the first rain upon the hills. The tall factory chimneys seemed trying to be taller than the mountain peaks ; as if this landscape were full (as its history has been full) of the very madness of ambition. The wage-slavery we live in is a wicked thing. But there is nothing in which the Scotch are more piercing and poetical, I might say more perfect, than in their Scotch wickedness. It is what makes the Master of Ballantrae the most thrilling of all fictitious villains. It is what makes the Master of Lovat the most thrilling of all historical villains. It is poetry.

It is an intensity which is on the edge of madness—or (what is worse) magic. Well, the Scotch have managed to apply something of this fierce romanticism even to the lowest of all lordships and serfdoms ; the proletarian inequality of to-day. You do meet now and then, in Scotland, the man you never meet anywhere else but in novels ; I mean the self-made man ; the hard, insatiable man, merciless to himself as well as to others. It is not " enterprise " ; it is kleptomania. He is quite mad, and a much more obvious public pest than any other kind of kleptomaniac ; but though he is a cheat, he is not an illusion. He does exist; I have met quite two of him. Him alone among modern merchants we do not weakly flatter when we call him a bandit. Something of the irresponsibility of the true dark ages really clings about him. Our scientific civilization is not a civilization ; it is a smoke nuisance. Like smoke it is choking us ; like smoke it will pass away. Only of one or two Scotsmen, in my experience, was it true that where there is smoke there is fire.

But there are other kinds of fire; and better. The one great advantage of this

strange national temper is that, from the beginning of all chronicles, it has provided resistance as well as cruelty. In Scotland nearly everything has always been in revolt'— especially loyalty. If these people are capable of making Glasgow, they are also capable of wrecking it ; and the thought of my many good friends in that city makes me really doubtful about which would figure in human memories as the more huge calamity of the two. In Scotland there are many rich men so weak as to call themselves strong. But there are not so many poor men weak enough to believe them.

As I came out of Glasgow I saw men standing about the road. They had little lanterns tied to the fronts of their caps, like the fairies who used to dance in the old fairy pantomimes. They were not, however, strictly speaking, fairies. They might have been called gnomes, since they worked in the chasms of those purple and chaotic hills. They worked in the mines from whence comes the fuel of our fires. Just at the moment when I saw them, moreover, they were not dancing ; nor were they working. They were doing nothing. Which, in my opinion (and I trust yours), was the finest thing they could do. 8 113

The Sectarian of Society

A FIXED creed is absolutely indispensable to A_ freedom. For while men are and should be various, there must be some communication between them if they are to get any pleasure out of their variety. And an intellectual formula is the only thing that can create a communication that does not depend on mere blood, class, or capricious sympathy. If we all start with the agreement that the sun and moon exist, we can talk about our different visions of them. The strong-eyed man can boast that he sees the sun as a perfect circle. The short-sighted man may say (or if he is an impressionist, boast) that he sees the moon as a silver blur. The colour-blind man may rejoice in the fairy-trick which enables him to live under a green sun and a blue moon. But if once it be held that there is nothing but a silver blur in one man's eye or a bright circle (like a monocle) in the other man's, then neither is free, for each is slmt up in the cell of a separate universe.

The Sectarian of Society

But, indeed, an even worse fate, practically considered, follows from the denial of the original intellectual formula. Not only does the individual become narrow, but he spreads narrowness across the world like a cloud ; he causes narrowness to increase and multiply like a weed. For what happens is this : that all the short-sighted people come together and build a city called Myopia, where they take short-sightedness for granted and paint shortsighted pictures and pursue very short-sighted policies. Meanwhile all the men who can stare at the sun get together on Salisbury Plain and do nothing but stare at the sun ; and all the men who see a blue moon band themselves together and assert the blue moon, not once in a blue moon, but incessantly. So that instead of a small and varied group, you have enormous monotonous groups. Instead of the liberty of dogma, you have the tyranny of taste.

Allegory apart, instances of what I mean will occur to every one ; perhaps the most obvious is Socialism. Socialism means the ownership by the organ of government (whatever it is) of all things necessary to production.

"5

A Miscellany of Men

If a man claims to be a Socialist in that sense he can be any kind of man he likes in any other sense—a bookie, a Mahatma, a man about town, an archbishop, a Margate nigger. Without recalling at the moment clear-headed Socialists in all of these capacities, it is obvious that a clear-headed Socialist (that is, a Socialist with a creed) can be a soldier, like Mr. Blatchford, or a Don, like Mr. Ball, or a Bath-chairman like Mr. Meek, or a clergyman like Mr. Conrad Noel, or an artistic tradesman like the late Mr. William Morris.

But some people call themselves Socialists, and will not be bound by what they call a narrow dogma ; they say that Socialism means far, far more than this ; all that is high, all that is free, all that is, etc. etc. Now mark their dreadful fate ; for they become totally unfit to be tradesmen, or soldiers, or clergymen, or any other stricken human thing, but become a particular sort of person who is always the same. When once it has been discovered that Socialism does not mean a narrow economic formula, it is also discovered that Socialism does mean wearing one particular kind of clothes, reading one particular kind of books, hanging up one particular kind of pictures, and in the majority of cases even 116

The Sectarian of Society

eating one particular kind of food. For men must recognize each other somehow. These men will not know each other by a principle, like fellow-citizens. They cannot know each other by a smell, like dogs. So they have to fall back on general colouring : on the fact that a man of their sort will have a wife in pale green and Walter Crane's " Triumph of Labour " hanging in the hall.

There are, of course, many other instances ; for modern society is almost made up of these large monochrome patches. Thus I, for one, regret the supersession of the old Puritan unity, founded on theology, but embracing all types from Milton to the grocer, by that newer Puritan unity which is founded rather on certain social habits, certain common notions, both permissive and prohibitive, in connexion with particular social pleasures.

Thus I, for one, regret that (if you are going to have an aristocracy) it did not remain a logical one founded on the science of heraldry : a thing asserting and defending the quite defensible theory that physical genealogy is the test ; instead of being, as it is now, a mere machine of Eton and Oxford for varnishing 117

anybody rich enough with one monotonous varnish.

And it is supremely so in the case of religion. As long as you have a creed, which every one in a certain group believes or is supposed to believe, then that group will consist of the old recurring figures of religious history, who can be appealed to by the creed and judged by it: the saint, the hypocrite, the brawler, the weak brother. These people do each other good ; or they all join together to do the hypocrite good, with heavy and repeated blows. But once break the bond of doctrine which alone holds these people together and each will gravitate to his own kind outside the group. The hypocrites will all get together and call each other saints ; the saints will get lost in a desert and call themselves weak brethren ; the weak brethren will get weaker and weaker in a general atmosphere of imbecility ; and the brawler will go off looking for somebody else with whom to brawl.

This has very largely happened to modern English religion; I have been in many churches, chapels, and halls where a confident pride in having got beyond creeds was coupled with quite a paralysed incapacity to get beyond catchwords. But wherever the falsity 118

appears it comes from neglect of the same truth : that men should agree on a principle, that they may differ on everything else ; that God gave men a law that they might turn it into liberties.

There was hugely more sense in the old people who said that a wife and husband ought to have the same religion than there is in all the contemporary gushing about sister souls and kindred spirits and auras of identical colour. As a matter of fact, the more the sexes are in violent contrast the less likely they are to be in violent collision. The more incompatible their tempers are the better. Obviously a wife's soul cannot possibly be a sister soul. It is very seldom so much as a first cousin. There are very few marriages of identical taste arid temperament; they are generally unhappy. But to have the same fundamental theory; to think the same thing a virtue, whether you practise or neglect it; to think the same thing a sin, whether you punish or pardon or laugh at it; in the last extremity to call the same thing duty and the same thing disgrace-—this really is necessary to a tolerably happy marriage ; and it is much 119

better represented by a common religion than it is by affinities and auras. And what applies to the family applies to the nation. A nation with a root religion will be tolerant. A nation with no religion will be bigoted. Lastly, the worst effect of all is this : that when men come together to profess a creed, they come courageously, though it is to hide in catacombs and caves. But when they come together in a clique they come sneakishly, eschewing all change or disagreement, though it is to dine to a brass band in a big London hotel. For birds of a feather flock together, but birds of the white feather most of all.

The Fool

FOR many years I had sought him, and at last I found him in a club. I had been told that he was everywhere; but I had almost begun to think that he was nowhere. I had been assured that there were millions of him ; but before my late discovery I inclined to think that there were none of him. After my late discovery I am sure that there is one ; and I incline to think that there are several, say, a few hundreds, but unfortunately most of them occupying important positions. When I say " him," I mean the entire idiot.

I have never been able to discover that " stupid public " of which so many literary men complain. The people one actually meets in trains or at tea-parties seem to me quite bright and interesting ; certainly quite enough so to call for the full exertion of one's own wits. And even when I have heard brilliant " conversationalists " conversing with other people, the conversation had much more equality and give and take than this age of 121

intellectual snobs will admit. I have sometimes felt tired, like other people ; but rather tired with men's talk and variety than with their stolidity or sameness ; therefore it was that I sometimes longed to find the refreshment of a single fool.

But it was denied me. Turn where I would I found this monotonous brilliancy of the general intelligence, this ruthless, ceaseless sparkle of humour and good sense. The " mostly fools " theory has been used in an anti-democratic sense ; but when I found at last my priceless ass, I did not find him in what is commonly called the democracy ; nor in the aristocracy cither. The man of the democracy generally talks quite rationally, sometimes on the anti-democratic side, but always with an idea of giving reasons for what he says and referring to the realities of his experience. Nor is it the aristocracy that is stupid; at least, not that section of the aristocracy which represents it in politics. They are often cynical, especially about money, but even their boredom tends to make them a little eager for any real information or originality. If a man like Mr. Winston Churchill or Mr. Wyndham made up his mind for any reason to attack Syndicalism he would find

The Fool

out what it was first. Not so the man I found in the club.

He was very well dressed ; he had a heavy but handsome face ; his black clothes suggested the City and his grey moustaches the Army ; but the whole suggested that he did not really belong to either, but was one of those who dabble in shares and who play at soldiers. There was some third element about him that was neither mercantile nor military. His manners were a shade too gentlemanly to be quite those of a gentleman. They involved an unction and over-emphasis of the club-man : and I suddenly remembered feeling the same thing in some old actors or old playgoers who had modelled themselves on actors. As I came in he said, " If I was the Government," and then put a cigar in his mouth which he lit carefully with long intakes of breath. Then he took the cigar out of his mouth again and said, " I'd give it 'em," as if it were quite a separate sentence. But even while his mouth was stopped with the cigar his companion or interlocutor leaped to his feet and said with great heartiness, snatching up a hat, " Well, I must be off. Tuesday ! " I dislike these 123 dark suspicions, but I certainly fancied I recognized the sudden geniality with which one takes leave of a bore.

When, therefore, he removed the narcotic stopper from his mouth it was to me that he addressed the belated epigram, " I'd give it 'em."

"What would you give them," I asked, *' the minimum wage ? "

" I'd give them beans," he said. " I'd shoot 'em down-—shoot 'em down, every man Jack of them. I lost my best train yesterday, and here's the whole country paralysed, and here's a handful of obstinate fellows standing between the country and coal. I'd shoot 'em down ! "

" That would surely be a little harsh," I pleaded. " After all, they are not under martial law, though I suppose two or three of them have commissions in the Yeomanry."

" Commissions in the Yeomanry! " he repeated, and his eyes and face, which became startling and separate, like those of a boiled lobster, made me feel sure that he had something of the kind himself.

" Besides," I continued, " wouldn't it be quite enough to confiscate their money ? "

" Well, I'd send them all to penal servitude, 124

The Fool

anyhow," he said, " and I'd confiscate their funds as well."

" The policy is daring and full of difficulty," I replied, " but I do not say that it is wholly outside the extreme rights of the republic. But you must remember that though the facts of property have become quite fantastic, yet the sentiment of property still exists. These coal-owners, though they have not earned the mines, though they could not work the mines, do quite honestly feel that they own the mines. Hence your suggestion of shooting them down, or even of confiscating their property, raises very-—•—

" What do you mean ? " asked the man with the cigar, with a bullying eye. " Who yer talking about ? "

"I'm talking about what you were talking about," I replied ; " as you put it so perfectly, about the handful of obstinate fellows who are standing between the country and the coal. I mean the men who are selling their own coal for fancy prices, and who, as long as they can get those prices, care as little for national starvation as most merchant princes and pirates have cared for the provinces that were wasted or the peoples that were enslaved just before their ships came home. But though I 125

am a bit of a revolutionist myself, I cannot quite go with you in the extreme violence you suggest. You say-— •—

" I say," he cried, bursting through my speech with a really splendid energy like that of some noble beast, " I say I'd take all these blasted miners and-—•— "

I had risen slowly to my feet, for I was profoundly moved ; and I stood staring at that mental monster.

" Oh," I said, " so it is the miners who are all to be sent to penal servitude, so that we may get more coal. It is the miners who are to be shot dead, every man Jack of them ; for if once they are all shot dead they will start mining again. . . . You must forgive me, sir ; I know I seem somewhat moved. . . . The fact is, I have just found something . . . something I have been looking for for years."

" Well," he asked, with no unfriendly stare, " and what have you found ? "

" No," I answered, shaking my head sadly, " I do not think it would be quite kind to tell you what I have found."

He had a hundred virtues, including the capital virtue of good humour, and we had no difficulty in changing the subject and forgetting the disagreement. He talked about 126

society, his town friends and his country sports, and I discovered in the course of it that he was a county magistrate, a Member of Parliament, and a director of several important companies. He was also that other thing, which I did not tell him.

The moral is that a certain sort of person does exist, to whose glory this article is dedicated. He is not the ordinary man. He is not the miner, who is sharp enough to ask for the necessities of existence. He is not the mine-owner, who is sharp enough to get a great deal more, by selling his coal at the best possible moment. He is not the aristocratic politician, who has a cynical but a fair sympathy with both economic opportunities. But he is the man who appears in scores of public places open to the upper middle class or (that less known but more powerful section) the lower upper class. Men like this all over the country are really saying whatever comes into their heads in their capacities of justice of the peace, candidate for Parliament, Colonel of the Yeomanry, old family doctor, Poor Law guardian, coroner, or, above all, arbiter in trade disputes. He suffers, in the literal sense, 127

from softening of the brain ; he has softened it by always taking the view of everything most comfortable for his country, his class, and his private personality. He is a deadly public danger. But as I have given him his name at the beginning of this article there is no need for me to repeat it at the end.

The Conscript and the Crisis ^> ^>

VERY few of us ever see the history of our own time happening. And I think the best service a modern journalist can do to society is to record as plainly as ever he can exactly what impression was produced on his mind by anything he has actually seen and heard on the outskirts of any modern problem or campaign. Though all he saw of a railway strike was a flat meadow in Essex in which a train was becalmed for an hour or two, he will probably throw more light on the strike by describing this which he has seen than by describing the steely kings of commerce and the bloody leaders of the mob whom he has never seen— nor any one else either. If he comes a day too late for the battle of Waterloo (as happened to a friend of my grandfather) he should still remember that a true account of the day after Waterloo would be a most valuable thing to have. Though he was on the wrong side of the door when Rizzio was being murdered, we should still like to have 9 "9

the wrong side described in the right way. Upon this principle I, who know nothing of diplomacy or military arrangements, and have only held my breath like the rest of the world while France and Germany were bargaining, will tell quite truthfully of a small scene I saw, one of the thousand scenes that were, so to speak, the ante-rooms of that inmost chamber of debate.

In the course of a certain morning I came into one of the quiet squares of a small French town and found its cathedral. It was one of those grey and rainy days which rather suit the Gothic. The clouds were leaden, like the solid blue-grey lead of the spires and the jewelled windows ; the sloping roofs and high-shouldered arches looked like cloaks drooping with damp ; and the stiff gargoyles that stood out round the walls were scoured with old rains and new. I went into the round, deep porch with many doors and found two grubby children playing there out of the rain. I also found a notice of services, etc., and among these I found the announcement that at

The Conscript and the Crisis

to say, the draft of young men who were being taken from their homes in that little town and sent to serve in the French Army ; sent (as it happened) at an awful moment, when the French Army was encamped at a parting of the ways. There were already a great many people there when I entered, not only of all kinds, but in all attitudes, kneeling, sitting, or standing about. And there was that general sense that strikes every man from a Protestant country, whether he dislikes the Catholic atmosphere or likes it; 1 mean, the general sense that the thing was " going on all the time " ; that it was not an occasion, but a perpetual process, as if it were a sort of mystical inn.

Several tricolours were hung quite near to the altar, and the young men, when they came in, filed up the church and sat right at the front. They were, of course, of every imaginable social grade ; for the French conscription is really strict and universal. Some looked like young criminals, some like young priests, some like both. Some were so obviously prosperous and polished that a barrack-room must seem to them like hell; others (by the look of them) had hardly ever been in so decent a place. But it was not so much the

A Miscellany of Men

mere class variety that most sharply caught an Englishman's eye. It was the presence of just those one or two kinds of men who would never have become soldiers in any other way. There are many reasons for becoming a soldier. It may be a matter of hereditary luck or abject hunger or heroic virtue or fugitive vice ; it may be an interest in the work or a lack of interest in any other work. But there would always be two or three kinds of people who would never tend to soldiering ; all those kinds of people were there. A lad with red hair, large ears, and very careful clothing, somehow announced across the church that he had always taken care of his health, not even from thinking about it, but simply because he was told, and that he was one of those who pass from childhood to manhood without any shock of being a man. In the row in front of him there was a very slight and vivid little Jew, of the sort that is a tailor and a Socialist. By one of those accidents that make real life so unlike anything else, he was the one of the company who seemed especially devout. Behind these stiff or sensitive boys were ranged the ranks of their mothers and fathers, with knots and bunches of their little brothers and sisters.

The Conscript and the Crisis

The children kicked their little legs, wriggled about the seats, and gaped at the arched roof while their mothers were on their knees praying their own prayers, and here and there crying. The grey clouds of rain outside gathered, I suppose, more and more ; for the deep church continuously darkened. The lads in front began to sing a military hymn in odd, rather strained voices; I could not disentangle the words, but only one perpetual refrain ; so that it sounded like

Sacrarterumbrrar pour la patrie, Valdarkararump pour la patrie.

Then this ceased ; and silence continued, the coloured windows growing gloomier and gloomier with the clouds. In the dead stillness a child started crying suddenly and incoherently. In a city far to the north a French diplomatist and a German aristocrat were talking.

I will not make any commentary on the thing that could blur the outline of its almost cruel actuality. I will not talk nor allow any one else to talk about " clericalism " and " militarism." Those who talk like that are made of the same mud 133

A Miscellany of Men

as those who call all the angers of the unfortunate " Socialism." The women who were calling in the gloom around me on God and the Mother of God were not " clericalists "; or, if they were, they had forgotten it. And I will bet my boots the young men were not " militarists "•—quite the other way just then. The priest made a short speech ; he did not utter any priestly dogmas (whatever they are), he uttered platitudes. In such circumstances platitudes are the only possible things to say; because they are true. He began by saying that he supposed a large number of them would be uncommonly glad not to go. They seemed to assent to this particular priestly dogma with even more than their alleged superstitious credulity. He said that war was hateful, and that we all hated it ; but that " in all things reasonable " the law of one's own commonwealth was the voice of God. He spoke about Joan of Arc, and how she had managed to be a bold and successful soldier while still preserving her virtue and practising her religion ; then he gave them each a little paper book. To which they replied (after a brief interval for reflection) :

Pongprongperesklang pour la patrie, Tambrangtararrone pour la patrie,

which I feel sure was the best and most pointed reply.

While all this was happening feelings quite indescribable crowded about my own darkening brain, as the clouds crowded above the darkening church. They were so entirely of the elements and the passions that I cannot utter them in an idea, but only in an image. It seemed to me that we were barricaded in this church, but we could not tell what was happening outside the church. The monstrous and terrible jewels of the windows darkened or glistened under moving shadow or light, but the nature of that light and the shapes of those shadows we did not know and hardly dared to guess. The dream began, I think, with a dim fancy that enemies were already in the town, and that the enormous oaken doors were groaning under their hammers. Then I seemed to suppose that the town itself had been destroyed by fire, and effaced, as it may be thousands of years hence, and that if I opened the door I should come out on a wilderness as flat and sterile as the sea. Then the vision behind the veil of stone and slate grew wilder with earthquakes. I seemed to sec chasms

cloven to the foundations of all things, and letting up an infernal dawn. Huge things happily hidden from us had climbed out of the abyss, and were striding about taller than the clouds. And when the darkness crept from the sapphires of Mary to the sanguine garments of St. John I fancied that some hideous giant was walking round the church and looking in at each window in turn.

Sometimes, again, I thought of that church with coloured windows as a ship carrying many lanterns struggling in a high sea at night. Sometimes I thought of it as a great coloured lantern itself, hung on an iron chain out of heaven and tossed and swung to and fro by strong wings, the wings of the princes of the air. But I never thought of it or the young men inside it save as something precious and in peril, or of the things outside but as something barbaric and enormous.

I know there are some who cannot sympathize with such sentiments of limitation ; I know there are some who would feel rio touch of the heroic tenderness if some day a young man, with red hair, large ears, and his mother's lozenges in his pocket, were found dead in uniform in the passes of the Vosges. But on this subject I have heard many philosophies 136

and thought a good deal for myself; and the conclusion I have come to is Sacrarterumbrrar pour la Patrie, and it is not likely that I shall alter it now.

But when I came out of the church there were none of these things, but only a lot of shops, including a paper-shop, selling papers which announced that the negotiations were proceeding satisfactorily.

The Miser and his Friends ^ <^ ^

IT is a sign of sharp sickness in a society when it is actually led by some special sort of lunatic. A mild touch of madness may even keep a man sane ; for it may keep him modest. So some exaggerations in the State may remind it of its own normal. But it is bad when the head is cracked ; when the roof of the commonwealth has a tile loose.

The two or three cases of this that occur in history have always been gibbeted gigantically. Thus Nero has become a black proverb, not merely because he was an oppressor, but because he was also an aesthete—— that is, an erotomaniac. He not only tortured other people's bodies ; he tortured his own soul into the same red revolting shapes. Though he came quite early in Roman Imperial history and was followed by many austere and noble emperors, yet for us the Roman Empire was never quite cleansed of that memory of the sexual madman. The populace or barbarians from whom we come could not forget the hour 138

The Miser and his Friends

when they came to the highest place of the earth, saw the huge pedestal of the earthly omnipotence, read on it Divus Causar, and looked up and saw a statue without a head.

It is the same with that ugly entanglement before the Renaissance, from which, alas, most memories of the Middle Ages are derived. Louis XI was a very patient and practical man of the world ; but (like many good business men) he was mad. The morbidity of the intriguer and the torturer clung about everything he did, even when it was right. And just as the great Empire of Antoninus and Aurelius never wiped out Nero, so even the silver splendour of the latter saints, such as Vincent de Paul, has never painted out for the British public the crooked shadow of Louis XI. Whenever the unhealthy man has been on top, he has left a horrible savour that humanity finds still in its nostrils. Now in our time the unhealthy man is on top ; but he is not the man mad on sex, like Nero ; or mad on statecraft, like Louis XI ; he is simply the man mad on money. Our tyrant is not the satyr or the torturer ; but the miser.

The modern miser has changed much from i39

A Miscellany of Men

the miser of legend and anecdote ; but only because he has grown yet more insane. The old miser had some touch of the human artist about him in so far that he collected gold—a substance that can really be admired for itself, like ivory or old oak. An old man who picked up yellow pieces had something of the simple ardour, something of the mystical materialism of a child who picks out yellow flowers. Gold is but one kind of coloured clay, but coloured clay can be very beautiful. The modern idolator of riches is content with far less genuine things. The glitter of guineas is like the glitter of buttercups, the chink of pelf is like the chime of bells, compared with the dreary papers and dead calculations which make the hobby of the modern miser.

The modern millionaire loves nothing so lovable as a coin. He is content sometimes with the dead crackle of notes ; but far more often with the mere repetition of noughts in a ledger, all as like each other as eggs to eggs. And as for comfort, the old miser could be comfortable, as many tramps and savages are, when he was once used to being unclean. A man could find some comfort in an unswept attic or an unwashed shirt. But the Yankee 140

The Miser and his Friends

millionaire can find no comfort with five telephones at his bed-head and ten minutes for his lunch. The round coins in the miser's stocking were safe in some sense. The round noughts in the millionaire's ledger are safe in no sense ; the same fluctuation which excites him with their increase depresses him with their diminution. The miser at least collects coins ; his hobby is numismatics. The man who collects noughts collects nothings.

It may be admitted that the man amassing millions is a bit of an idiot; but it may be asked in what sense does he rule the modern world. The answer to this is very important and rather curious. The evil enigma for us here is not the rich, but the Very Rich. The distinction is important; because this special problem is separate from the old general quarrel about rich and poor that runs through the Bible and all strong books, old and new. The special problem to-day is that certain powers and privileges have grown so worldwide and unwieldy that they are out of the power of the moderately rich as well as of the moderately poor. They are out of the power of everybody except a few 141

millionaires—that is, misers. In the old normal friction of normal wealth and poverty I am myself on the Radical side. I think that a Berkshire squire has too much power over his tenants ; that a Brompton builder has too much power over his workmen ; that a West London doctor has too much power over the poor patients in the West London Hospital.

But a Berkshire squire has no power over cosmopolitan finance, for instance. A Brompton builder has not money enough to run a Newspaper Trust. A West End doctor could not make a corner in quinine and freeze everybody out. The merely rich are not rich enough to rule the modern market. The things that change modern history, the big national and international loans, the big educational and philanthropic foundations, the purchase of numberless newspapers, the big prices paid for peerages, the big expenses often incurred in elections—these are getting too big for everybody except the misers : the men with the largest of earthly fortunes and the smallest of earthly aims.

There are two other odd and rather important things to be said about them. The first is this : that with this aristocracy we do not have the chance of a lucky variety in types 142

The Miser and his Friends

which belongs to larger and looser aristocracies. The moderately rich include all kinds of people—even good people. Even priests are sometimes saints ; and even soldiers are sometimes heroes. Some doctors have really grown wealthy by curing their patients and not by flattering them ; some brewers have been known to sell beer. But among the Very Rich you will never find a really generous man, even by accident. They may give their money away, but they will never give themselves away ; they are egoistic, secretive, dry as old bones. To be smart enough to get all that money you must be dull enough to want it.

Lastly, the most serious point about them is this : that the new miser is flattered for his meanness and the old one never was. It was never called self-denial in the old miser that he lived on bones. It is called self-denial in the new millionaire if he lives on beans. A man like Dancer was never praised as a Christian saint for going in rags. A man like Rockefeller is praised as a sort of pagan stoic for his early rising or his unassuming dress. His " simple " meals, his " simple " clothes, his " simple " funeral, are all extolled as if they

were creditable to him. They are disgraceful to him : exactly as disgraceful as the tatters and vermin of the old miser were disgraceful to him. To be in rags for charity would be the condition of a saint; to be in rags for money was that of a filthy old fool. Precisely in the same way, to be " simple " for charity is the state of a saint; to be " simple " for money is that of a filthy old fool. Of the two I have more respect for the old miser, gnawing bones in an attic : if he was not nearer to God, he was at least a little nearer to men. His simple life was a little more like the life of the real poor.

The Mystagogue ^x ^ -Q> ^x

WHENEVER you hear much of things being unutterable and indefinable and impalpable and unnamable and subtly indescribable, then elevate your aristocratic nose towards heaven and snuff up the smell of decay. It is perfectly true that there is something in all good things that is beyond all speech or figure of speech. But it is also true that there is in all good things a perpetual desire for expression and concrete embodiment ; and though the attempt to embody it is always inadequate, the attempt is always made. If the idea does not seek to be the word, the chances are that it is an evil idea. If the word is not made flesh it is a bad word. Thus Giotto or Fra Angelico would have at once admitted theologically that God was too good to be painted ; but they would always try to paint Him. And they felt (very rightly) that representing Him as a rather quaint old man with a gold crown and a white beard, like a king of the elves, was less profane than re-10 145

sisting the sacred impulse to express Him in some way. That is why the Christian world is full of gaudy pictures and twisted statues which seem, to many refined persons, more blasphemous than the secret volumes of an atheist. The trend of good is always towards Incarnation. But, on the other hand, those refined thinkers who worship the Devil, whether in the swamps of Jamaica or the salons of Paris, always insist upon the shapelessness, the wordlessness, the unutterable character of the abomination. They call him " horror of emptiness," as did the black witch in Stevenson's Dynamiter; they worship him as the unspeakable name, as the unbearable silence. They think of him as the void in the heart of the whirlwind ; the cloud on the brain of the maniac; the toppling turrets of vertigo or the endless corridors of nightmare. It was the Christians who gave the Devil a grotesque and energetic outline, with sharp horns and spiked tail. It was the saints who drew Satan as comic and even lively. The Satanists never drew him at all.

And as it is with moral good and evil, so it is also with mental clarity and mental confu-
146

sion. There is one very valid test by which we may separate genuine, if perverse and unbalanced, originality and revolt from mere impudent innovation and bluff. The man who really thinks he has an idea will always try to explain that idea. The charlatan who has no idea will always confine himself to explaining that it is much too subtle to be explained. The first idea may really be very outree or specialist; it may really be very difficult to express to ordinary people. But because the man is trying to express it, it is most probable that there is something in it, after all. The honest man is he who is always trying to utter the unutterable, to describe the indescribable ; but the quack lives not by plunging into mystery, but by refusing to come out of it.

Perhaps this distinction is most comically plain in the case of the thing called Art, and the people called Art Critics. It is obvious that an attractive landscape or a living face can only half express the holy cunning that has made them what they are. It is equally obvious that a landscape painter expresses only half of the landscape ; a portrait painter

only half of the person ; they are lucky if they express so much. And again it is yet more obvious that any literary description of the pictures can only express half of them, and that the less important half. Still, it does express something ; the thread is not broken that connects God with Nature, or Nature with men, or men with critics. The " Mona Lisa " was in some respects (not all, I fancy) what God meant her to be. Leonardo's picture was, in some respects, like the lady. And Walter Pater's rich description was, in some respects, like the picture. Thus we come to the consoling reflection that even literature, in the last resort, can express something other than its own unhappy self.

Now the modern critic is a humbug, because he professes to be entirely inarticulate. Speech is his whole business ; and he boasts of being speechless. Before Botticelli he is mute. But if there is any good in Botticelli (there is much good, and much evil too) it is emphatically the critic's business to explain it; to translate it from terms of painting into terms of diction. Of course, the rendering will be inadequate'—but so is Botticelli. It is a 148

The Mystagogue

fact he would be the first to admit. But anything which has been intelligently received can at least be intelligently suggested. Pater does suggest an intelligent cause for the cadaverous colour of Botticelli's " Venus Rising from the Sea." Ruskin does suggest an intelligent motive for Turner destroying forests and falsifying landscapes. These two great critics were far too fastidious for my taste ; they urged to excess the idea that a sense of art was a sort of secret to be patiently taught and slowly learnt. Still, they thought it could be taught: they thought it could be learnt. They constrained themselves, with considerable creative fatigue, to find the exact adjectives which might parallel in English prose what has been done in Italian painting. The same is true of Whistler and R. A. M. Stevenson and many others in the exposition of Velasquez. They had something to say about the pictures ; they knew it was unworthy of the pictures, but they said it.

Now the eulogists of the latest artistic insanities (Cubism and Post-Impressionism and Mr. Picasso) are eulogists and nothing else. They are not critics ; least of all creative 149

A Miscellany of Men

critics. They do not attempt to translate beauty into language ; they merely tell you that it is untranslatable——that is, unutterable, indefinable, indescribable, impalpable, ineffable, and all the rest of it. The cloud is their banner : they cry to chaos and old night. They circulate a piece of paper on which Mr. Picasso has had the misfortune to upset the ink and tried to dry it with his boots, and they seek to terrify democracy by the good old anti-democratic muddlements : that " the public " does not understand these things ; that " the likes of us " cannot dare to question the dark decisions of our lords.

I venture to suggest that we resist all this rubbish by the very simple test mentioned above. If there were anything intelligent in such art, something of it at least could be made intelligible in literature. Man is made with one head, not with two or three. No criticism of Rembrandt is as good as Rembrandt ; but it can be so written as to make a man go back and look at his pictures. If there is a curious and fantastic art, it is the business of the art critics to create a curious and fantastic literary expression for it; inferior to it, doubtless, but still akin to it. If they cannot do this, as they cannot; if 150

The Mystagogue

there is nothing in their eulogies, as there is nothing except eulogy—then they are quacks or the high-priests of the unutterable. If the art critics can say nothing about the artists except that they are good it is because the artists are bad. They can explain nothing because they have found nothing ; and they have found nothing because there is nothing to be found.

THE one case for Revolution is that it is the only quite clean and complete road to anything —even to restoration. Revolution alone can be not merely a revolt of the living, but also a resurrection of the dead.

A friend of mine was once walking down the street in a town of Western France, situated in that area that used to be called La Vendee ; which in that great creative crisis about 1790 formed a separate and mystical soul of its own, and made a revolution against a revolution. As my friend went down this street he whistled an old French air which he had found, like Mr. Gandish, " in his researches into 'istry," and which had somehow taken his fancy ; the song to which those last sincere loyalists went into battle. I think the words ran :• —

Monsieur d'Charette a dit a ceux d'Ancenis,
Mes amis ! Le roi va ramener la Fleur de Lys.
My friend was (and is) a Radical, but he was
The Red Reactionary

(and is) an Englishman, and it never occurred to him that there could be any harm in singing archaic lyrics out of remote centuries ; that one had to be a Catholic to enjoy the " Dies Irae," or a Protestant to remember " Lilli-bullero." Yet he was stopped and gravely warned that things so politically provocative might get him at least into temporary trouble.

A little time after I was helping King George V to get crowned, by walking round a local bonfire and listening to a local band. Just as a bonfire cannot be too big, so (by my theory of music) a band cannot be too loud, and this band was so loud, emphatic, and obvious, that I actually recognized one or two of the tunes. And I noticed that quite a formidable proportion of them were Jacobite tunes ; that is, tunes that had been primarily meant to keep George V out of his throne for ever. Some of the real airs of the old Scottish rebellion were played, such as " Charlie is My Darling," or " What's a' the steer, kimmer ? " songs that men had sung while marching to destroy and drive out the monarchy under which we live. They were songs in which the very kinsmen of the present King were swept aside as usurpers. They were songs in which

A Miscellany of Men

the actual words " King George " occurred as a curse and a derision. Yet they were played to celebrate his very Coronation ; played as promptly and innocently as if they had been " Grandfather's Clock " or " Rule Britannia " or " The Honeysuckle and the Bee."

That contrast is the measure, not only between two nations, 1 but between two modes of historical construction and development. For there is not really very much difference, as European history goes, in the time that has elapsed between us and the Jacobite and between us and the Jacobin. When George III was crowned the gauntlet of the King's Champion was picked up by a partisan of the Stuarts. When George III was still on the throne the Bourbons were driven out of France as the Stuarts had been driven out of England. Yet the French are just sufficiently aware that the Bourbons might possibly return that they will take a little trouble to discourage it ; whereas we are so certain that the Stuarts will never return that we actually play their most passionate tunes as a compliment to their rivals. And we do not even do it tauntingly. I examined the faces of all the

The Red Reactionary

bandsmen ; and I am sure they were devoid of irony : indeed, it is difficult to blow a wind instrument ironically. We do it quite unconsciously ; because we have a huge fundamental dogma, which the French have not. We really believe that the past is past. It is a very doubtful point.

Now the great gift of a revolution (as in France) is that it makes men free in the past as well as free in the future. Those who have cleared away everything could, if they liked, put back everything. But we who have preserved everything — we cannot restore anything. Take, for the sake of argument, the complex and many-coloured ritual of the Coronation recently completed. That rite is stratified with the separate centuries; from the first rude need of discipline to the last fine shade of culture or corruption, there is nothing that cannot be detected or even dated. The fierce and childish vow of the lords to serve their lord " against all manner of folk " obviously comes from the real Dark Ages ; no longer confused, even by the ignorant, with the Middle Ages. It comes from some chaos of Europe, when there was one old Roman road

across four of our counties ; and when hostile " folk " might live in the next village. The sacramental separation of one man to be the friend of the fatherless and the nameless belongs to the true Middle Ages ; with their great attempt to make a moral and invisible Roman Empire ; or (as the Coronation Service says) to set the cross for ever above the ball. Elaborate local tomfooleries, such as that by which the Lord of the Manor of Worksop is alone allowed to do something or other, these probably belong to the decay of the Middle Ages, when that great civilization died out in grotesque literalism and entangled heraldry. Things like the presentation of the Bible bear witness to the intellectual outburst at the Reformation; things like the Declaration against the Mass bear witness to the great wars of the Puritans ; and things like the allegiance of the Bishops bear witness to the wordy and parenthetical political compromises which (to my deep regret) ended the wars of religion.

But my purpose here is only to point out one particular thing. In all that long list of variations there must be, and there are, things which energetic modern minds would really wish, with the reasonable modification, to 156

restore. Dr. Clifford would probably be glad to see again the great Puritan idealism that forced the Bible into an antique and almost frozen formality. Dr. Horton probably really regrets the old passion that excommunicated Rome. In the same way Mr. Belloc would really prefer the Middle Ages ; as Lord Rose-bcry would prefer the Erastian oligarchy of the eighteenth century. The Dark Ages would probably be disputed (from widely different motives) by Mr. Rudyard Kipling and Mr. Cunninghame Graham. But Mr. Cunning-hame Graham would win.

But the black case against Conservative (or Evolutionary) politics is that none of these sincere men can win. Dr. Clifford cannot get back to the Puritans ; Mr. Belloc cannot get back to the mediscvals ; because (alas!) there has been no Revolution to leave them a clear space for building or rebuilding. Frenchmen have all the ages behind them, and can wander back and pick and choose. But Englishmen have all the ages on top of them, and can only lie groaning under that imposing tower, without being able to take so much as a brick out of it. If the French decide that

their Republic is bad they can get rid of it; but if we decide that a Republic was good, we should have much more difficulty. If the French democracy actually desired every detail of the mediaeval monarchy, they could have it. I do not think they will or should, but they could. If another Dauphin were actually crowned at Rheims ; if another Joan of Arc actually bore a miraculous banner before him ; if mediaeval swords shook and blazed in every gauntlet; if the golden lilies glowed from every tapestry; if this were really proved to be the will of France and the purpose of Providence—such a scene would still be the lasting and final justification of the

French Revolution.

For no such scene could conceivably have happened under Louis XVI.

The Separatist and Sacred Things ^>

IN the very laudable and fascinating extensions of our interest in Asiatic arts or faiths, there are two incidental injustices which we tend nowadays to do to our own records and our own religion. The first is a tendency to talk as if certain things were not only present in the higher Orientals, but were peculiar to them. Thus our magazines will fall into a habit of wondering praise of Bushido, the Japanese chivalry, as if no Western knights had ever vowed noble vows, or as if no Eastern knights had ever broken them. Or again, our drawing-rooms will be full of the praises of Indian renunciation and Indian unworldliness, as if no Christians had been saints, or as if all Buddhists had been. But if the first injustice is to think of human virtues as peculiarly Eastern, the other injustice is a failure to appreciate what really is peculiarly Eastern. It is too much taken for granted that the Eastern sort of idealism is certainly superior and convincing ;

whereas in truth it is only separate and peculiar. All that is richest, deepest, and subtlest in the East is rooted in Pantheism ; but all that is richest, deepest, and subtlest in us is concerned with denying passionately that Pantheism is either the highest or the purest religion.

Thus, in turning over some excellent books recently written on the spirit of Indian or Chinese art and decoration, I found it quietly and curiously assumed that the artist must be at his best if he flows with the full stream of Nature; and identifies himself with all things ; so that the stars are his sleepless eyes and the forests his far-flung arms. Now in this way of talking both the two injustices will be found. In so far as what is claimed is a strong sense of the divine in all things, the Eastern artists have no more monopoly of it than they have of hunger and thirst.

I have no doubt that the painters and poets of the Far East do exhibit this ; but I rebel at being asked to admit that we must go to the Far East to find it. Traces of such sentiments can be found, I fancy, even in other painters and poets. I do not question that the poet Wo Wo (that ornament of the eighth dynasty) may have written the words : 1 60

The Separatist and Sacred Things

" Even the most undignified vegetable is for this person capable of producing meditations not to be exhibited by much weeping." But I do not therefore admit that a Western gentleman named Wordsworth (who made a somewhat similar remark) had plagiarised from Wo Wo, or was a mere Occidental fable and travesty of that celebrated figure. I do not deny that Tinishona wrote that exquisite example of the short Japanese poem entitled " Honourable Chrysanthemum in Honourable Hole in Wall." But I do not therefore admit that Tennyson's little verse about the flower in the cranny was not original and even sincere.

It is recorded (for all I know) of the philanthropic Emperor Bo, that when engaged in cutting his garden lawn with a mower made of alabaster and chrysoberyl, he chanced to cut down a small flower ; whereupon, being much affected, he commanded his wise men immediately to take down upon tablets of ivory the lines beginning : " Small and unobtrusive blossom with ruby extremities." But this incident, touching as it is, does not shake my belief in the incident of Robert Burns and the daisy ; and I am left with an impression that poets are pretty much the n 161

A Miscellany of Men

same everywhere in their poetry— and in their prose.

I have tried to convey my sympathy and admiration for Eastern art and its admirers, and if I have not conveyed them I must give it up and go on to more general considerations. I therefore proceed to say-— with the utmost respect, that it is Cheek, a rarefied and etherealized form of Cheek, for this school to speak in this way about the mother that bore them, the great civilization of the West. The West also has its magic landscapes, only through our incurable materialism they look like landscapes as well as like magic. The West also has its symbolic figures, only they look like men as well as symbols. It will be answered (and most justly) that Oriental art ought to bs free to follow its own instinct and tradition ; that its artists are concerned to suggest one thing and our artists another ; that both should be admired in their difference. Profoundly true ; but what is the difference ? It is certainly not as the Orientalisers assert, that we must go to the Far East for a sympathetic and transcendental interpretation of Nature. We have paid a long enough toll of mystics and even of madmen to be quit of that disability.

The Separatist and Sacred Things

Yet there is a difference, and it is just what I suggested. The Eastern mysticism is an ecstasy of unity; the Christian mysticism is an ecstasy of creation, that is, of separation and mutual surprise. The latter says, like St. Francis, " My brother fire and my sister water " ; the former says, " Myself fire and myself water." Whether you call the Eastern attitude an extension of oneself into everything or a contraction of- oneself into nothing is a matter of metaphysical definition. The effect is the same, an effect which lives and throbs throughout all the exquisite arts of the East. This effect is the thing called rhythm, a pulsation of pattern, or of ritual, or of colours, or of cosmic theory, but always suggesting the unification of the individual with the world.

But there is quite another kind of sympathy —the sympathy with a thing because it is different. No one will say that Rembrandt did not sympathize with an old woman; but no one will say that Rembrandt painted like an old woman. No one will say that Reynolds did not appreciate children ; but no one will say he did it childishly. The supreme instance of this divine division is sex, and that explains (what I could never understand in my youth) why Christendom 163

A Miscellany of Men

called the soul the bride of God. For real love is an intense realization of the " separate-ness " of all our souls. The most heroic and human love-poetry of the world is never mere passion; precisely because mere passion really is a melting back into Nature, a meeting of the waters. And water is plunging and powerful ; but it is only powerful downhill. The high and human love-poetry is all about division rather than, identity ; and in the great love-poems even the man as he embraces the woman sees her, in the same instant, afar off— a virgin and a stranger.

For the first injustice, of which we have spoken, still recurs ; and if we grant that the East has a right to its difference, it is not realized in what we differ. That nursery tale from nowhere about St. George and the Dragon really expresses best the relation between the West and the East. There were many other differences, calculated to arrest even the superficial eye, between a saint and a dragon. But the essential difference was simply this : that the Dragon did want to eat St. George ; whereas St. George would have felt a strong distaste for eating the Dragon. In most of the stories he killed the Dragon. In many of the stories he not only 164

The Separatist and Sacred Things

spared, but baptized it. But in neither case did the Christian have any appetite for cold dragon. The Dragon, however, really has an appetite for cold Christian'—and especially for cold Christianity. This blind intention to absorb, to change the shape of everything and digest it in the darkness of a dragon's stomach ; this is what is really meant by the Pantheism and Cosmic Unity of the East. The Cosmos as such is cannibal; as old Time ate his children. The Eastern saints were saints because they wanted to be swallowed up. The Western saint, like St. George, was sainted by the Western Church precisely because he refused to be swallowed. The same process of thought that has prevented nationalities disappearing in Christendom has prevented the complete appearance of Pantheism. All Christian men instinctively resist the idea of being absorbed into an Empire ; an Austrian, a Spanish, a British, or a Turkish Empire. But there is one empire, much larger and much more tyrannical, which free men will resist with even stronger passion. The free man violently resists being absorbed into the empire which is called the Universe. He demands Home Rule for his nationality, but still more Home Rule for his 165

A Miscellany of Men

home. Most of all he demands Home Rule for himself. He claims the right to be saved, in spite of Moslem fatalism. He claims the right to be damned in spite of theosophical optimism. He refuses to be the Cosmos; because he refuses to forget it.

The Mummer <^ <N, <^ ^ o

THE night before Christmas Eve I heard a burst of musical voices so close that they might as well have been inside the house instead of just outside; so I asked them inside, hoping that they might then seem farther away. Then I realized that they were the Christmas Mummers, who come every year in country parts to enact the rather rigid fragments of the old Christmas play of St. George, the Turkish Knight, and the Very Venal Doctor. I will not describe it ; it is indescribable ; but I will describe my parallel sentiments as it passed.

One could see something of that half-failure that haunts our artistic revivals of mediaeval dances, carols, or Bethlehem Plays. There are elements in all that has come to us from the more morally simple society of the Middle Ages : elements which moderns, even when they are medievalists, find it hard to understand and harder to imitate. The first is the 167

A Miscellany of Men

primary idea of Mummery itself. If you will observe a child just able to walk, you will see that his first idea is not to dress up as anybody •—but to dress up. Afterwards, of course, the idea of being the King or Uncle William will leap to his lips. But it is generally suggested by the hat he has already let fall over his nose, from far deeper motives. Tommy does not assume the hat primarily because it is Uncle William's hat, but because it is not Tommy's hat. It is a ritual investiture ; and is akin to those Gorgon masks that stiffened the dances of Greece or those towering mitres that came from the mysteries of Persia. For the essence of such ritual is a profound paradox : the concealment of the personality combined with the exaggeration of the person. The man performing a rite seeks to be at once invisible and conspicuous. It is part of that divine madness which all other creatures wonder at in Man, that he alone parades this pomp of obliteration and anonymity. Man is not, perhaps, the only creature who dresses himself, but he is the only creature who disguises himself. Beasts and birds do indeed take the colours of their environment; but that is not in order to be watched, but in order not to be watched ; it is not the formalism of rejoicing, 168

The Mummer

but the formlessness of fear. It is not so with men, whose nature is the unnatural. Ancient Britons did not stain themselves blue because they lived in blue forests ; nor did Georgian beaux and belles powder their hair to match an Arctic landscape ; the Britons were not dressing up as kingfishers nor the beaux pretending to be polar bears. Nay, even when modern ladies paint their faces a bright mauve, it is doubted by some naturalists whether they do it with the idea of escaping notice. So merry-makers (or Mummers) adopt their costume to heighten and exaggerate their own bodily presence and identity ; not to sink it, primarily speaking, in another identity. It is not Acting—that comparatively low profession • — comparatively I mean. It is Mummery ; and, as Mr. Kensit would truly say, all elaborate religious ritual is Mummery. That is, it is the noble conception of making Man something other and more than himself when he stands at the limit of human things. It is only careful faddists and feeble German philosophers who want to wear no clothes : and be " natural " in their Dionysian revels. Natural men, really vigorous and exultant men, want to wear more and more clothes when they are revelling. They want worlds of 169

waistcoats and forests of trousers and pagodas of tall hats toppling up to the stars.

Thus it is with the lingering Mummers at Christmas in the country. If our more refined revivers of Miracle Plays or Morris Dances tried to reconstruct the old Mummers' Play of St. George and the Turkish Knight (I do not know why they do not) they would think at once of picturesque and appropriate dresses. St. George's panoply would be pictured from the best books of armour and blazonry : the Turkish Knight's arms and ornaments would be traced from the finest Saracenic arabesques. When my garden door opened on Christmas Eve and St. George of England entered, the appearance of that champion was slightly different. His face was energetically blacked all over with soot, above which he wore an aged and very tall top hat; he wore his shirt outside his coat like a surplice, and he flourished a thick umbrella. Now do not, I beg you, talk about " ignorance " ; or suppose that the Mummer in question (he is a very pleasant Rat-catcher, with a tenor voice) did this because he knew no better. Try to realize that even a Rat-catcher knows St. George of 170

England was not black, and did not kill the Dragon with an umbrella. The Rat-catcher is not under this delusion ; any more than Paul Veronese thought that very good men have luminous rings round their heads ; any more than the Pope thinks that Christ washed the feet of the twelve in a Cathedral; any more than the Duke of Norfolk thinks the lions on a tabard are like the lions at the Zoo. These things are denaturalised because they are symbols ; because the extraordinary occasion must hide or even disfigure the ordinary people. Black faces were to mediaeval mummeries what carved masks were to Greek plays : it was called being " vizarded." My Ratcatcher is not sufficiently arrogant to suppose for a moment that he looks like St. George. But he is sufficiently humble to be convinced that if he looks as little like himself as he can, he will be on the right road.

This is the soul of Mumming ; the ostentatious secrecy of men in disguise. There are, of course, other mediaeval elements in it which are also difficult to explain to the fastidious mediaevalists of to-day. There is, for instance, a certain output of violence into the void. It 171

can best be defined as a raging thirst to knock men down without the faintest desire to hurt them. All the rhymes with the old ring have the trick of turning on everything in which the rhymsters most sincerely believed, merely for the pleasure of blowing off steam in startling yet careless phrases. When Tennyson says that King Arthur " drew all the petty princedoms under him," and " made a realm and ruled, "his grave Royalism is quite modern. Many medisevals, outside the mediaeval republics, believed in monarchy as solemnly as Tennyson. But that older verse^—

When good King Arthur ruled this land He was a goodly King-He stole three pecks of barley-meal To make a bag-pudding, is far more Arthurian than anything in The Idylls of the King. There are other elements ; especially that sacred thing that can perhaps be called Anachronism. All that to us is Anachronism was to mediaevals merely Eternity. But the main excellence of the Mumming Play lies still, I think, in its uproarious secrecy. If we cannot hide our hearts in healthy darkness, at least we can hide our faces in healthy blacking. If you cannot escape like a philosopher into a forest, at least you can carry the forest with 172

you, like a Jack-in-the-Green. It is well to walk under universal ensigns ; and there is an old tale of a tyrant to whom a walking forest was the witness of doom. That, indeed, is the very intensity of the notion : a masked man is ominous : but who shall face a mob of masks ?

The Aristocratic 'Any <^ ^> ^>- ^

THE Cheap Tripper, pursued by the curses of the aesthetes and the antiquaries, really is, I suppose, a symptom of the strange and almost unearthly ugliness of our diseased society. The costumes and customs of a hundred peasantries are there to prove that such ugliness does not necessarily follow from mere poverty, or mere democracy, or mere unlettered simplicity of mind.

But though the tripper, artistically considered, is a sign of our decadence, he is not one of its worst signs, but relatively one of its best; one of its most innocent and most sincere. Compared with many of the philosophers and artists who denounce him, he looks like a God-fearing fisher or a noble mountaineer. His antics with donkeys and concertinas, crowded char-a-bancs, and exchanged hats, though clumsy, are not so vicious

or even so fundamentally vulgar as many of the amusements of the over-educated. People are not more crowded on a char-a-banc than they are at a political " At Home," or even an artistic soiree ; and if the female trippers are overdressed, at least they are not overdressed and underdressed at the same time. It is better to ride a donkey than to be a donkey. It is better to deal with the Cockney festival which asks men and women to change hats, rather than with the modern Utopia that wants them to change heads.

But the truth is that such small, but real, element of vulgarity as there is indeed in the tripper, is part of a certain folly and falsity which is characteristic of much modernity, and especially of the very people who persecute the poor tripper most. There is something in the whole society, and even especially in the cultured part of it, that does things in a clumsy and unbeautiful way.

A case occurs to me in the matter of Stone-henge, which I happened to visit lately. Now to a person really capable of feeling the poetry of Stonehenge it is almost a secondary

matter whether he sees Stonehenge at all. The vast void roll of the empty land towards Salisbury, the grey tablelands like primeval altars, the trailing rain - clouds, the vapour of primeval sacrifices, would all tell him of a very ancient and very lonely Britain. It would not spoil his Druidic mood if he missed Stonehenge. But it does spoil his mood to find Stonehenge——surrounded by a brand-new fence of barbed wire, with a policeman and a little shop selling picture post-cards.

Now if you protest against this, educated people will instantly answer you, " Oh, it was done to prevent the vulgar trippers who chip stones and carve names and spoil the look of Stonehenge." It does not seem to occur to them that barbed wire and a policeman rather spoil the look of Stonehenge. The scratching of a name, particularly when performed with a blunt penknife or pencil by a person of imperfect School Board education, can be trusted in a little while to be indistinguishable from the greyest hieroglyphic by the grandest Druid of old. But nobody could get a modern policeman into the same picture with a Druid. This really vital piece of vandalism was done by the educated, not the uneducated ; it was done by the influence of the artists or anti-176

quaries who wanted to preserve the antique beauty of Stonehenge. It seems to me curious to preserve your lady's beauty from freckles by blacking her face all over ; or to protect the pure whiteness of your wedding garment by dyeing it green.

And if you ask, "But what else could any one have done, what could the most artistic age have done to save the monument ? " I reply, " There are hundreds of things that Greeks or Mediaevals might have done ; and I have no notion what they would have chosen ; but I say that by an instinct in their whole society they would have done something that was decent and serious and suitable to the place. Perhaps some family of knights or warriors would have the hereditary duty of guarding such a place. If so their armour would be appropriate; their tents would be appropriate ; not deliberately •— they would grow like that. Perhaps some religious order such as normally employ nocturnal watches and the relieving of guard would protect such a place. Perhaps it would be protected by all sorts of rituals, consecrations, or curses, which would seem to you mere raving superstition and silliness. But they do not seem to me one-twentieth part so silly, from a purely

rationalist point of view, as calmly making a spot hideous in order to keep it beautiful."

The thing that is really vulgar, the thing that is really vile, is to live in a good place without living by its life. Any one who settles down in a place without becoming part of it is (barring peculiar personal cases, of course) a tripper or wandering cad. For instance, the Jew is a genuine peculiar case. The Wandering Jew is not a wandering cad. He is a highly civilized man in a highly difficult position ; the world being divided, and his own nation being divided, about whether he can do anything else except wander.

The best example of the cultured, but common, tripper is the educated Englishman on the Continent. We can no longer explain the quarrel by calling Englishmen rude and foreigners polite. Hundreds of Englishmen are extremely polite, and thousands of foreigners are extremely rude. The truth of the matter is that foreigners do not resent the rude Englishman. What they do resent, what they do most justly resent, is the polite Englishman. He visits Italy for Botticellis or Flanders for Rembrandts, and he treats 178

the great nations that made these things courteously— as he would treat the custodians of any museum. It does not seem to strike him that the Italian is not the custodian of the pictures, but the creator of them. He can afford to look down on such nations—when he can paint such pictures.

That is, in matters of art and travel, the psychology of the cad. If, living in Italy, you admire Italian art while distrusting Italian character, you are a tourist, or cad. If, living in Italy, you admire Italian art while despising Italian religion, you are a tourist, or cad. It does not matter how many years you have lived there. Tourists will often live a long time in hotels without discovering the nationality of the waiters. Englishmen will often live a long time in Italy without discovering the nationality of the Italians. But the test is simple. If you admire what Italians did without admiring Italians — you are a cheap tripper.

The same, of course, applies much nearer

home. I have remarked elsewhere that
country shopkeepers are justly offended by
London people, who, coming among them,

continue to order all their goods from London. It is caddish to wink and squint at the colour of a man's wine, like a wine-taster ; and then refuse to drink it. It is equally caddish to wink and squint at the colour of a man's orchard, like a landscape painter ; and then refuse to buy the apples. It is always an insult to admire a thing and not use it. But the main point is that one has no right to see Stonehenge without Salisbury Plain and Salisbury. One has no right to respect the dead Italians without respecting the live ones. One has no right to visit a Christian society like a diver visiting the deep-sea fishes-— fed along a lengthy tube by another atmosphere, and seeing the sights without breathing the air. It is very real bad manners.

The New Theologian *o *o *o -^

IT is an old story that names do not fit things ; it is an old story that the oldest forest is called the New Forest, and that Irish stew is almost peculiar to England. But these are traditional titles that tend, of their nature, to stiffen ; it is the tragedy of to-day that even phrases invented for to-day do not fit it. The forest has remained new while it is nearly a thousand years old ; but our fashions have grown old while they were still new.

The extreme example of this is that when modern wrongs are attacked, they are almost always attacked wrongly. People seem to have a positive inspiration for finding the inappropriate phrase to apply to an offender ; they are always accusing a man of theft when he has been convicted of murder. They must accuse Sir Edward Carson of outrageous rebellion, when his offence has really been a sleek submission to the powers that be. They must describe Mr. Lloyd George as using his 181

eloquence to rouse the mob, whereas he has really shown considerable cleverness in damping it down. It was probably under the same impulse towards a mysterious misfit of names that people denounced Dr. Inge as " the Gloomy Dean."

Now there is nothing whatever wrong about being a Dean ; nor is there anything wrong about being gloomy. The only question is what dark but sincere motives have made you gloomy. What dark but sincere motives have made you a Dean. Now the address of Dr. Inge which gained him this erroneous title was mostly concerned with a defence of the modern capitalists against the modern strikers, from whose protest he appeared to anticipate appalling results. Now if we look at the facts about that gentleman's depression and also about his Deanery, we shall find a very curious state of things.

When Dr. Inge was called " the Gloomy Dean " a great injustice was done him. He had appeared as the champion of our capitalist community against the forces of revolt; and any one who does that exceeds in optimism rather than pessimism. A man who really thinks that strikers have suffered no wrong, or that employers have done no wrong'—such 182

a man is not a Gloomy Dean, but a quite wildly and dangerously happy Dean. A man who can feel satisfied with modern industrialism must be a man with a mysterious fountain of high spirits. And the actual occasion is not less curious ; because, as far as I can make out, his title to gloom reposes on his having said that our workers demand high wages, while the placid people of the Far East will quite cheerfully work for less.

This is true enough, of course, and there does not seem to be much difficulty about the matter. Men of the Far East will submit to very low wages for the same reason that they will submit to " the punishment known as Li, or Slicing " ; for the same reason that they will praise polygamy and suicide ; for the same reason that they subject the wife utterly to the husband or his parents ; for the same reason that they serve their temples with prostitutes for priests ; for the same reason that they sometimes seem to make no distinction between sexual passion and sexual perversion. They do it, that is, because they are Heathens ; men with traditions different from ours about the limits of endurance and the gestures of self-respect. They may be very much better than we are in hundreds of other 183

A Miscellany of Men

Ways ; and I can quite understand a man (though hardly a Dean) really preferring their historic virtues to those of Christendom. A man may perhaps feel more comfortable among his Asiatic coolies than among his European comrades : and as we are to allow the Broadest Thought in the Church, Dr. Inge has as much right to his heresy as anybody else. It is true that, as Dr. Inge says, there are numberless Orientals who will do a great deal of work for very little money ; and it is most undoubtedly true that there are several high-placed and prosperous Europeans who like to get work done and pay as little as possible for it.

But I cannot make out why, with his enthusiasm for heathen habits and traditions, the Dean should wish to spread in the East the ideas which he has found so dreadfully unsettling in the West. If some thousands of years of paganism have produced the patience and industry that Dean Inge admires, and if some thousand years of Christianity have produced the sentimentality and sensationalism which he regrets, the obvious deduction is that Dean Inge would be much happier if he were a heathen Chinee. Instead of supporting Christian missions to Korea or Japan, he 184

The New Theologian

ought to be at the head of a great mission in London for converting the English to Taoism or Buddhism. There his passion for the moral beauties of paganism would have free and natural play ; his style would improve ; his mind would begin slowly to clear ; and he would be free from all sorts of little irritating scrupulosities which must hamper even the most Conservative Christian in his full praise of sweating and the sack.

In Christendom he will never find rest. The perpetual public criticism and public change which is the note of all our history springs from a certain spirit far too deep to be defined. It is deeper than democracy; nay, it may often appear to be non-democratic ; for it may often be the special defence of a minority or an individual. It will often leave the ninety-and-nine in the wilderness and go after that which is lost. It will often risk the State itself to right a single wrong ; and do justice though the heavens fall. Its highest expression is not even in the formula of the great gentlemen of the French Revolution who said that all men were free and equal. Its 185

A Miscellany of Men

highest expression is rather in the formula of the peasant who said that a man's a man for a' that. If there were but one slave in England, and he did all the work while the rest of us made merry, this spirit that is in us would still cry aloud to God night and day. Whether or no this spirit was produced by, it clearly works with, a creed which postulates a humanized God and a vividly personal immortality. Men must not be busy merely like a swarm, or even happy merely like a herd ; for it is not a question of men, but of a man. A man's meals may be poor, but they must not be bestial; there must always be that about the meal which permits of its comparison to the sacrament. A man's bed may be hard, but it must not be abject or unclean : there must always be about the bed something of the decency of the death-bed.

This is the spirit which makes the Christian poor begin their terrible murmur whenever there is a turn of prices or a deadlock of toil that threatens them with vagabondage or pauperization ; and we cannot encourage the Dean with any hope that this spirit can be cast out. Christendom will continue to suffer all the disadvantages of being Christian : it is the Dean who must be gently but firmly 186

altered. He had absent-mindedly strayed into the wrong continent and the wrong creed. I advise him to chuck it.

But the case is more curious still. To connect the Dean with Confucian temples or traditions may have appeared fantastic ; but it is not. Dr. Inge is not a stupid old Tory Rector, strict both on Church and State. Such a man might talk nonsense about the Christian Socialists being " court chaplains of King Demos " or about his own superb valour in defying the democracy that rages in the front pews of Anglican churches. We should not expect a mere old-fashioned country clergyman to know that Demos has never been king in England and precious seldom anywhere else ; we should not expect him to realize that if King Demos had any chaplains they would be uncommonly poorly paid. But Dr. Inge is not old-fashioned; he considers himself highly progressive and advanced. He is a New Theologian; that is, he is liberal in theology——and nothing else. He is apparently in sober fact, and not as in any fantasy, in sympathy with those who would soften the 187

superior claim of our creed by urging the rival creeds of the East; with those who would absorb the virtues of Buddhism or of Islam. He holds a high seat in that modern Parliament of Religions where all believers respect each others' unbelief.

Now this has a very sharp moral for modern religious reformers. When next you hear the " liberal " Christian say that we should take what is best in Oriental faiths, make quite sure what are the things that people like Dr. Inge call best ; what are the things that people like Dr. Inge propose to take. You will not find them imitating the military valour of the Moslem. You will not find them imitating the miraculous ecstasy of the Hindoo. The more you study the " broad " movement of to-day, the more you will find that these people want something much less like Chinese metaphysics, and something much more like Chinese Labour. You will find the levelling of creeds quite unexpectedly close to the lowering of wages. Dr. Inge is the typical latitudi-narian of to-day ; and was never more so than when he appeared not as the apostle of the blacks, but as the apostle of the blacklegs. Preached, as it is, almost entirely among the prosperous and polite, our brotherhood with iSS

Buddhism or Mohammedanism practically means this——that the poor must be as meek as Buddhists, while the rich may be as ruthless as Mohammedans. That is what they call the reunion of all religions.

The Romantic in the Rain <^> ^ <^

THE middle classes of modern England are quite fanatically fond of washing ; and are often enthusiastic for teetotalism. I cannot therefore comprehend why it is that they exhibit a mysterious dislike of rain. Rain, that inspiring and delightful thing, surely combines the qualities of these two ideals with quite a curious perfection. Our philanthropists are eager to establish public baths everywhere. Rain surely is a public bath ; it might almost be called mixed bathing. The appearance of persons coming fresh from this great natural lustration is not perhaps polished or dignified; but for the matter of that, few people are dignified when coming out of a bath. But the scheme of rain in itself is one of an enormous purification. It realizes the dream of some insane hygienist: it scrubs the sky. Its giant brooms and mops seem to reach the starry rafters and starless corners of the cosmos ; it is a cosmic spring-cleaning.

The Romantic in the Rain

If the Englishman is really fond of cold baths, he ought not to grumble at the English climate for being a cold bath. In these days we are constantly told that we should leave our little special possessions and join in the enjoyment of common social institutions and a common social machinery. I offer the rain as a thoroughly Socialistic institution. It disregards that degraded delicacy which has hitherto led each gentleman to take his shower-bath in private. It is a better shower-bath, because it is public and communal; and, best of all, because somebody else pulls the string.

As for the fascination of rain for the water drinker, it is a fact the neglect of which I simply cannot comprehend. The enthusiastic water drinker must regard a rainstorm as a sort of universal banquet and debauch of his own favourite beverage. Think of the imaginative intoxication of the wine drinker if the crimson clouds sent down claret or the golden clouds hock. Paint upon primitive darkness some such scenes of apocalypse, towering and gorgeous skyscapes in which champagne falls like fire from heaven or the dark skies grow purple and tawny with the

191

A Miscellany of Men

terrible colours of port. All this must the wild abstainer feel, as he rolls in the long soaking grass, kicks his ecstatic heels to heaven, and listens to the roaring rain. It is he, the water drinker, who ought to be the true bacchanal of the forests ; for all the forests are drinking water. Moreover, the forests are apparently enjoying it: the trees rave and reel to and fro like drunken giants ; they clash boughs as revellers clash cups ; they roar undying thirst and howl the health of the world.

All around me as I write is a noise of Nature drinking : and Nature makes a noise when she is drinking, being by no means refined. If I count it Christian mercy to give a cup of cold water to a sufferer, shall I complain of these multitudinous cups of cold water handed round to all living things ; a cup of water for every shrub ; a cup of water for every weed ? I would be ashamed to grumble at it. As Sir Philip Sidney said, their need is greater than mine—especially for water.

There is a wild garment that still carries nobly the name of a wild Highland clan : a clan come from those hills where rain is not

The Romantic in the Rain

so much an incident as an atmosphere. Surely every man of imagination must feel a tempestuous flame of Celtic romance spring up within him whenever he puts on a mackintosh. I could never reconcile myself to carrying an umbrella ; it is a pompous Eastern business, carried over the heads of despots in the dry, hot lands. Shut up, an umbrella is an unmanageable walking-stick; open, it is an inadequate tent. For my part, I have no taste for pretending to be a walking pavilion ; I think nothing of my hat, and precious little of my head. If I am to be protected against wet, it must be by some closer and more careless protection, something that I can forget altogether. It might be a Highland plaid. It might be that yet more Highland thing, a mackintosh.

And there is really something in the mackintosh of the military qualities of the Highlander. The proper cheap mackintosh has a blue and white sheen as of steel or iron ; it gleams like armour. I like to think of it as the uniform of that ancient clan in some of its old and misty raids. I like to think of all the Macintoshes, in their mackintoshes, descending on some doomed Lowland village, their wet waterproofs flashing in the sun or moon. For 13 X 93

indeed this is one of the real beauties of rainy weather, that while the amount of original and direct light is commonly lessened, the number of things that reflect light is unquestionably increased. There is less sunshine ; but there are more shiny things ; such beautifully shiny things as pools and puddles and mackintoshes. It is like moving in a world of mirrors.

And indeed this is the last and not the least gracious of the casual works of magic wrought by rain : that while it decreases light, yet it doubles it. If it dims the sky, it brightens the earth. It gives the roads (to the sympathetic eye) something of the beauty of Venice. Shallow lakes of water reiterate every detail of earth and sky ; we dwell in a double universe. Sometimes walking upon bare and lustrous pavements, wet under numerous lamps, a man seems a black blot on all that golden looking-glass, and could fancy he was flying in a yellow sky. But wherever trees and towns hang head downwards in a pigmy puddle, the sense of Celestial topsy-turvydom is the same. This bright, wet, dazzling confusion of shape and shadow, of reality and 194

The Romantic in the Rain

reflection, will appeal strongly to any one with the transcendental instinct about this dreamy and dual life of ours. It will always give a man the strange sense of looking down at the skies.

WHEN, as lately, events have happened that seem (to the fancy, at least) to test if not stagger the force of official government, it is amusing to ask oneself what is the real weakness of civilization, ours especially, when it contends with the one lawless man. I was reminded of one weakness this morning in turning over an old drawerful of pictures.

This weakness in civilization is best expressed by saying that it cares more for science than for truth. It prides itself on its " methods" more than its results; it is satisfied with precision, discipline, good communications, rather than with the sense of reality. But there are precise falsehoods as well as precise facts. Discipline may only mean a hundred men making the same mistake at the same minute. And good communications may in practice be very like those evil communications which are said to corrupt good manners. Broadly, we have reached a " scientific age," which wants to know whether 196

The False Photographer

the train is in the time-table, but not whether the train is in the station. I take one instance in our police inquiries that I happen to have come across : the case of photography.

Some years ago a poet of considerable genius tragically disappeared, and the authorities or the newspapers circulated a photograph of him, so that he might be identified. The photograph, as I remember it, depicted or suggested a handsome, haughty, and somewhat pallid man with his head thrown back, with long distinguished features, colourless thin hair and slight moustache, and though conveyed merely by the head and shoulders, a definite impression of height. If I had gone by that photograph, I should have gone about looking for a long soldierly but listless man, with a profile rather like the Duke of Connaught's.

Only, as it happened, I knew the poet personally ; I had seen him a great many times, and he had an appearance that nobody could possibly forget, if seen only once. He had the mark of those dark and passionate Westland Scotch, who before Burns and after have given many such dark eyes and dark emotions to the world. But in him the unmistakable

A Miscellany of Men

strain, Gaelic or whatever it is, was accentuated almost to oddity ; and he looked like some swarthy elf. He was small, with a big head and a crescent of coal-black hair round the back of a vast dome of baldness. Immediately under his eyes his cheekbones had so high a colour that they might have been painted scarlet; three black tufts, two on the upper lip and one under the lower, seemed to touch up the face with the fierce moustaches of Mephistopheles. His eyes had that " dancing madness " in them which Stevenson saw in the Gaelic eyes of Alan Breck ; but he sometimes distorted the expression by screwing a monstrous monocle into one of them. A man more unmistakable would have been hard to find. You could have picked him out in any crowd—so long as you had not seen his photograph.

But in this scientific picture of him twenty causes, accidental and conventional, had combined to obliterate him altogether. The limits of photography forbade the strong and almost melodramatic colouring of cheek and eyebrow. The accident of the lighting took nearly all the darkness out of the hair and made him look almost like a fair man. The framing and limitation of the shoulders 198

The False Photographer

made him look like a big man ; and the devastating bore of being photographed when you want to write poetry made him look like a lazy man. Holding his head back, as people do when they are being photographed (or shot), but as he certainly never held it normally, accidentally concealed the bald dome that dominated his slight figure. Here we have a clockwork picture, begun and finished by a button and a box of chemicals, from which every projecting feature has been more delicately and dexterously omitted than they could have been by the most namby-pamby flatterer, painting in the weakest water-colours on the smoothest ivory.

I happen to possess a book of Mr. Max Beerbohm's caricatures, one of which depicts the unfortunate poet in question. To say it represents an utterly incredible hobgoblin is to express in faint and inadequate language the licence of its sprawling lines. The authorities thought it strictly safe and scientific to circulate the poet's photograph. They would have clapped me in an asylum if I had asked them to circulate Max's caricature. But the caricature would have been far more likely to find the man.

A Miscellany of Men

This is a small but exact symbol of the failure of scientific civilization. It is so satisfied in knowing it has a photograph of a man that it never asks whether it has a likeness of him. Thus declarations, seemingly most detailed, have flashed along the wires of the world ever since I was a boy. We were told that in some row Boer policemen had shot an Englishman, a British subject, an English citizen. A long time afterwards we were quite casually informed that the English citizen was quite black. Well, it makes no difference to the moral question ; black men should be shot on the same ethical principles as white men. But it makes one distrust scientific communications which permitted so startling an alteration of the photograph. I am sorry we got hold of a photographic negative in which a black man came out white. Later we were told that an Englishman had fought for the Boers against his own flag, which would have been a disgusting thing to do. Later, it was admitted that he was an Irishman ; which is exactly as different as if he had been a Pole. Common sense, with all the facts before it, does see that black is not white, and that a nation that has never submitted has a right to moral independence. But why does it so 200

The False Photographer

seldom have all the facts before it ? Why are the big aggressive features, such as blackness or the Celtic wrath, always left out in such official communications, as they were left out in the photograph ? My friend the poet had hair as black as an African and eyes as fierce as an Irishman ; why does our civilization drop all four of the facts ? Its error is to omit the arresting thing — which might really arrest the criminal. It strikes first the chilling note of science, demanding a man " above the middle height, chin shaven, with grey moustache," etc., which might mean Mr. Balfour or Sir Redvers Buller. It does not seize the first fact of impression, as that a man is obviously a sailor or a Jew or a drunkard or a gentleman or a nigger or an albino or a prizefighter or an imbecile or an American. These are the realities by which the people really recognize each other. They are almost always left out of the inquiry.

r I ""HERE is one deep defect in our exten-J_ sion of cosmopolitan and Imperial cultures. That is, that in most human things if you spread your butter far you spread it thin. But there is an odder fact yet : rooted in something dark and irrational in human nature. That is, that when you find your butter thin, you begin to spread it. And it is just when you find your ideas wearing thin in your own mind that you begin to spread them among your fellow-creatures. It is a paradox ; but not my paradox. There are numerous cases in history ; but I think the strongest case is this. That we have Imperialism in all our clubs at the very time when we have Orientalism in all our drawing-rooms.

I mean that the colonial ideal of such men as Cecil Rhodes did not arise out of any fresh creative idea of the Western genius, it was a fad, and like most fads an imitation. For

what was wrong with Rhodes was not that, like Cromwell or Hildebrand, he made huge mistakes, nor even that he committed great crimes. It was that he committed these crimes and errors in order to spread certain ideas. And when one asked for the ideas they could not be found. Cromwell stood for Calvinism, Hildebrand for Catholicism : but Rhodes had no principles whatever to give to the world. He had only a hasty but elaborate machinery for spreading the principles that he hadn't got. What he called his ideals were the dregs of a Darwinism which had already grown not only stagnant, but poisonous. That the fittest must survive, and that any one like himself must be the fittest; that the weakest must go to the wall, and that any one he could not understand must be the weakest; that was the philosophy which he lumberingly believed through life, like many another agnostic old bachelor of the Victorian era. All his views on religion (reverently quoted in the Review of Reviews) were simply the stalest ideas of his time. It was not his fault, poor fellow, that he called a high hill somewhere in South Africa " his church." It was not his fault, I mean, that he could not see that a church all to oneself is not a church at all. It 203

A Miscellany of Men

is a madman's cell. It was not his fault that he " figured out that God meant as much of the planet to be Anglo-Saxon as possible." Many evolutionists much wiser had " figured out " things even more babyish. He was an honest and humble recipient of the plodding popular science of his time ; he spread no ideas that any cockney clerk in Streatham could not have spread for him. But it was exactly because he had no ideas to spread that he invoked slaughter, violated justice, and ruined republics to spread them.

But the case is even stronger and stranger. Fashionable Imperialism not only has no ideas of its own to extend ; but such ideas as it has are actually borrowed from the brown and black peoples to whom it seeks to extend them. The Crusading kings and knights might be represented as seeking to spread Western ideas in the East. But all that our Imperialist aristocrats could do would be to spread Eastern ideas in the East. For that very governing class which urges Occidental Imperialism has been deeply discoloured with Oriental mysticism and Cosmology.

The same society lady who expects the 204

Hindoos to accept her view of politics has herself accepted their view of religion. She wants first to steal their earth, and then to share their heaven. The same Imperial cynic who wishes the Turks to submit to English science has himself submitted to Turkish philosophy, to a wholly Turkish view of despotism and destiny.

There is an obvious and amusing proof of this in a recent life of Rhodes. The writer admits with proper Imperial gloom the fact that Africa is still chiefly inhabited by Africans. He suggests Rhodes in the South confronting savages and Kitchener in the North facing Turks, Arabs, and Soudanese, and then he quotes this remark of Cecil Rhodes : " It is inevitable fate that all this should be changed ; and I should like to be the agent of fate." That was Cecil Rhodes's one small genuine idea; and it is an Oriental idea.

Here we have evident all the ultimate idiocy of the present Imperial position. Rhodes and Kitchener are to conquer Moslem bedouins and barbarians, in order to teach them to believe only in inevitable fate. We are to wreck provinces and pour blood like Niagara, all in 205

Q»!

A Miscellany of Men

order to teach a Turk to say " Kismet " ; which he has said since his cradle. We are to deny Christian justice and destroy international equality, all in order to teach an Arab to believe he is " an agent of fate," when he has never believed anything else. If Cecil Rhodes's vision could come true (which fortunately is increasingly improbable), such countries as Persia or Arabia would simply be filled with ugly and vulgar fatalists in billycocks, instead of with graceful and dignified fatalists in turbans. The best Western idea, the idea of spiritual liberty and danger, of a doubtful and romantic future in which all things may happen—this essential Western idea Cecil Rhodes could not spread, because (as he says himself) he did not believe in it.

It was an Oriental who gave to Queen Victoria the crown of an Empress in addition to that of a Queen. He did not understand that the title of King is higher than that of Emperor. For in the East titles are meant to be vast and wild ; to be extravagant poems : the Brother of the Sun and Moon, the Caliph who lives for ever. But a King of England (at least in the days of real kings) did not bear a merely poetical title ; but rather a religious one. He belonged to his people and not merely 206

The Sultan

they to him. He was not merely a conqueror, but a father—yes, even when he was a bad father. But this sort of solid sanctity always goes with local affections and limits : and the Cecil Rhodes Imperialism set up not the King, but the Sultan ; with all the typically Eastern ideas of the magic of money, of luxury without uproar ; of prostrate provinces and a chosen race. Indeed, Cecil Rhodes illustrated almost every quality essential to the Sultan, from the love of diamonds to the scorn of woman.

The Architect of Spears ^> -^ ^

THE other day, in the town of Lincoln, I suffered an optical illusion which accidentally revealed to me the strange greatness of the Gothic architecture. Its secret is not, I think, satisfactorily explained in most of the discussions on the subject. It is said that the Gothic eclipses the classical by a certain richness and complexity, at once lively and mysterious. This is true; but Oriental decoration is equally rich and complex, yet it awakens a widely different sentiment. No man ever got out of a Turkey carpet the emotions that he got from a cathedral tower. Over all the exquisite ornament of Arabia and India there is the presence of something stiff and heartless, of something tortured and silent. Dwarfed trees and crooked serpents, heavy flowers and hunchbacked birds accentuate by the very splendour and contrast of their colour the servility and monotony of their shapes. It is like the vision of a sneering sage, who sees the whole universe as a pattern. 208

Certainly no one ever felt like this about Gothic, even if he happens to dislike it. Or, again, some will say that it is the liberty of the Middle Ages in the use of the comic or even the coarse that makes the Gothic more interesting than the Greek. There is more truth in this ; indeed, there is real truth in it. Few of the old Christian cathedrals would have passed the Censor of Plays. We talk of the inimitable grandeur of the old cathedrals ; but indeed it is rather their gaiety that we do not dare to imitate. We should be rather surprised if a chorister suddenly began singing "Bill Bailey" in church. Yet that would be only doing in music what the mediaevals did in sculpture. They put into a Miserere seat the very scenes that we put into a music-hall song : comic domestic scenes similar to the spilling of the beer and the hanging out of the washing. But though the gaiety of Gothic is one of its features, it also is not the secret of its unique effect. We see a domestic topsy-turvydom in many Japanese sketches. But delightful as these are, with their fairy tree-tops, paper houses, and toddling, infantile inhabitants, the pleasure they give is of a kind quite different from the joy and energy of the gargoyles. Some have even been so shallow 14 209

and illiterate as to maintain that our pleasure in mediaeval building is a mere pleasure in what is barbaric, in what is rough, shapeless, or crumbling like the rocks. This can be dismissed after the same fashion ; South Sea idols, with painted eyes and radiating bristles, are a delight to the eye ; but they do not affect it in at all the same way as Westminster Abbey. Some again (going to another and almost equally foolish extreme) ignore the coarse and comic in medievalism ; and praise the pointed arch only for its utter purity and simplicity, as of a saint with his hands joined in prayer. Here, again, the uniqueness is missed. There are Renaissance things (such as the ethereal silvery drawings of Raphael), there are even pagan things (such as the Praying Boy) which express as fresh and austere a piety. None of these explanations explain. And I never saw what was the real point about Gothic till I came into the town of Lincoln, and saw it behind a row of furniture-vans.

I did not know they were furniture-vans ; at the first glance and in the smoky distance I thought they were a row of cottages. A low stone wall cut off the wheels, and the vans were somewhat of the same colour as the yellowish clay or stone of the buildings around

them. I had come across that interminable Eastern plain which is like the open sea, and all the more so because the one small hill and tower of Lincoln stands up in it like a lighthouse. I had climbed the sharp, crooked streets up to this ecclesiastical citadel; just in front of me was a flourishing and richly coloured kitchen garden; beyond that was the low stone wall; beyond that the row of vans that looked like houses ; and beyond and above that, straight and swift and dark, light as a flight of birds, and terrible as the Tower of Babel, Lincoln Cathedral seemed to rise out of human sight.

As I looked at it I asked myself the questions that I have asked here ; what was the soul in all those stones ? They were varied, but it was not variety; they were solemn, but it was not solemnity ; they were farcical, but it was not farce. What is it in them that thrills and soothes a man of our blood and history, that is not there in an Egyptian pyramid or an Indian temple or a Chinese pagoda ? All of a sudden the vans I had mistaken for cottages began to move away to the left. In the start this gave to my eye and mind I really fancied that the Cathedral was moving towards the right. The two huge towers seemed to start

striding across the plain like the two legs of some giant whose body was covered with the clouds. Then I saw what it was.

The truth about Gothic is, first, that it is alive, and second, that it is on the march. It is the Church Militant; it is the only fighting architecture. All its spires are spears at rest; and all its stones are stones asleep in a catapult. In that instant of illusion, I could hear the arches clash like swords as they crossed each other. The mighty and numberless columns seemed to go swinging by like the huge feet of imperial elephants. The graven foliage wreathed and blew like banners going into battle ; the silence was deafening with all the mingled noises of a military march ; the great bell shook down, as the organ shook up its thunder. The thirsty-throated gargoyles shouted like trumpets from all the roofs and pinnacles as they passed ; and from the lectern in the core of the cathedral the eagle of the awful evangelist clashed his wings of brass.

And amid all the noises I seemed to hear the voice of a man shouting in the midst like one ordering regiments hither and thither in the fight; the voice of the great half - military master-builder; the architect of spears. I sould almost fancy he wore armour while he

made that church ; and I knew indeed that, under a scriptural figure, he had borne in either hand the trowel and the sword.

I could imagine for the moment that the whole of that house of life had marched out of the sacred East, alive and interlocked, like an army. Some Eastern nomad had found it solid and silent in the red circle of the desert. He had slept by it as by a world-forgotten pyramid ; and been woke at midnight by the wings of stone and brass, the tramping of the tall pillars, the trumpets of the waterspouts. On such a night every snake or sea-beast must have turned and twisted in every crypt or corner of the architecture. And the fiercely coloured saints marching eternally in the flamboyant windows would have carried their glorioles like torches across dark lands and distant seas ; till the whole mountain of music and darkness and lights descended roaring on the lonely Lincoln hill. So for some hundred and sixty seconds I saw the battle-beauty of the Gothic ; then the last furniture-van shifted itself away ; and I saw only a church tower in a quiet English town, round which the English birds were floating.

' I ^HERE is a fact at the root of all realities -L to - day which cannot be stated too simply. It is that the powers of this world are now not trusted simply because they are not trustworthy. This can be quite clearly seen and said without any reference to our several passions or partisanships. It does not follow that we think such a distrust a wise sentiment to express ; it does not even follow that we think it a good sentiment to entertain. But such is the sentiment, simply because such is the fact. The distinction can be quite easily defined in an example. I do not think that private workers owe an indefinite loyalty to their employer. But I do think that patriotic soldiers owe a more or less indefinite loyalty to their leader in battle. But even if they ought to trust their captain, the fact remains that they often do not trust him ; and the fact remains that he often is not fit to be trusted.

Most of the employers and many of the 214

Socialists seem to have got a very muddled ethic about the basis of such loyalty ; and perpetually try to put employers and officers upon the same disciplinary plane. I should have thought myself that the difference was alphabetical enough. It has nothing to do with the idealizing of war or the materializing of trade; it is a distinction in the primary purpose. There might be much more elegance and poetry in a shop under William Morris than in a regiment under Lord Kitchener. But the difference is not in the persons or the atmosphere, but in the aim. The British Army does not exist in order to pay Lord Kitchener. William Morris's shop, however artistic and philanthropic, did exist to pay William Morris. If it did not pay the shopkeeper it failed as a shop ; but Lord Kitchener does not fail if he is underpaid, but only if he is defeated. The object of the Army is the safety of the nation from one particular class of perils ; therefore, since all citizens owe loyalty to the nation, all citizens who are soldiers owe loyalty to the Army. But nobody has any obligation to make some particular rich man richer. A man is bound, of course, to consider the indirect results of his action in a strike ; but he is bound to consider that 215

A Miscellany of Men

in a swing, or a giddy-go-round, or a smoking concert ; in his wildest holiday or his most private conversation. But direct responsibility like that of a soldier he has none. He need not aim solely and directly at the good of the shop ; for the simple reason that the shop is not aiming solely and directly at the good of the nation. The shopman is, under decent restraints, let us hope, try ing to get what he can out of the nation ; the shop assistant may, under the same decent restraints, get what he can out of the shopkeeper. All this distinction is very obvious. At least I should have thought so.

But the primary point which I mean is this. That even if we do take the military view of mercantile service, even if we do call the rebellious shop assistant " disloyal "•— that leaves exactly where it was the question of whether he is, in point of fact, in a good or bad shop. Granted that all Mr. Poole's employees are bound to follow for ever the cloven pennon of the Perfect Pair of Trousers, it is all the more true that the pennon may, in point of fact, become imperfect. Granted that all Barney Barnato's workers ought to have 216

The Man on Top

followed him to death or glory, it is still a perfectly legitimate question to ask which he was likely to lead them to. Granted that Dr. Sawyer's boy ought to die for his master's medicines, we may still hold an inquest to find out if he died of them. While we forbid the soldier to shoot the general, we may still wish the general were shot.

The fundamental fact of our time is the failure of the successful man. Somehow we have so arranged the rules of the game that the winners are worthless for other purposes ; they can secure nothing except the prize. The very rich are neither aristocrats nor self-made men ; they are accidents-—or rather calamities. All revolutionary language is ageneration behind the times in talking of their futility. A revolutionist would say (with perfect truth) that coal-owners know next to nothing about coal-mining. But we are past that point. Coal-owners know next to nothing about coal-owning. They do not develop and defend the nature of their own monopoly with any consistent and courageous policy, however wicked, as did the old aristocrats with the monopoly of land. They 217

A Miscellany of Men

have not the virtues nor even the vices of tyrants; they have only their powers. It is the same with all the powerful of to-day ; it is the same, for instance, with the high-placed and high-paid official. Not only is the judge not judicial, but the arbiter is not even arbitrary. The arbiter decides, not by some gust of justice or injustice in his soul like the old despot dooming men under a tree, but by the permanent climate of the class to which he happens to belong. The ancient wig of the judge is often indistinguishable from the old wig of the flunkey.

To judge about success or failure one must see things very simply ; one must see them in masses, as the artist, half closing his eyes against details, sees light and shade. That is the only way in which a just judgment can be formed as to whether any departure or development, such as Islam or the American Republic, has been a benefit upon the whole. Seen close, such great erections always abound in ingenious detail and impressive solidity ; it is only by seeing them afar off that one can tell if the Tower leans.

Now if we thus take in the whole tilt or 218

posture of our modern state, we shall simply see this fact; that those classes who have on the whole governed, have on the whole failed. If you go to a factory you will see some very wonderful wheels going round ; you will be told that the employer often comes there early in the morning ; that he has great organizing power ; that if he works over the colossal accumulation of wealth he also works over its wise distribution. All this may be true of many employers, and it is practically said of all.

But if we shade our eyes from all this dazzle of detail; if we simply ask what has been the main feature, the upshot, the final fruit of the capitalist system, there is no doubt about the answer. The special and solid result of the reign of the employers has been—unemployment. Unemployment not only increasing, but becoming at last the very pivot upon which the whole process turns.

Or, again, if you visit the villages that depend on one of the great squires, you will hear praises, often just, of the landlord's good sense or good nature ; you will hear of whole systems of pensions or of care for the sick, like those of a small and separate nation ; you will see much cleanliness, order, and business 219

habits in the offices and accounts of the estate. But if you ask again what has been the upshot, what has been the actual result of the reign of landlords, again the answer is plain. At the end of the reign of landlords men will not live on the land. The practical effect of having landlords is not having tenants. The practical effect of having employers is that men are not employed. The unrest of the populace is therefore more than a murmur against tyranny; it is against a sort of treason. It is the suspicion that even at the top of the tree, even in the seats of the mighty, our very success is unsuccessful.

The Other Kind of Man -cy ^ ^x

THERE are some who are conciliated by Conciliation Boards. There are some who, when they hear of Royal Commissions, breathe again-— or snore again. There are those who look forward to Compulsory Arbitration Courts as to the islands of the blest. These men do not understand the day that they look upon or the sights that their eyes have seen.

The almost sacramental idea of representation, by which the few may incarnate the many, arose in the Middle Ages, and has done great things for justice and liberty. It has had its real hours of triumph, as when the States General met to renew France's youth like the eagle's ; or when all the virtues of the Republic fought and ruled in the figure of Washington. It is not having one of its hours of triumph now. The real democratic unrest at this moment is not an extension of the representative process, but rather a revolt against it. It is no good giving those now in revolt more boards and committees

and compulsory regulations. It is against these very things that they are revolting. Men are not only rising against their oppressors, but against their representatives— or, as they would say, their misrcpresentatives. The inner and actual spirit of workaday England is coming out not in applause, but in anger, as a god who should come out of his tabernacle to rebuke and confound his priests.

There is a certain kind of man whom we see many times in a day, but whom we do not, in general, bother very much about. He is the kind of man of whom his wife says that a better husband when he's sober you couldn't have. She sometimes adds that he never is sober ; but this is in anger and exaggeration. Really he drinks much less and works much more than the modern legend supposes. But it is quite true that he has not the horror of bodily outbreak, natural to the classes that contain ladies ; and it is quite true that he never has that alert and inventive sort of industry natural to the classes from which men can climb into great wealth. He has grown, partly by necessity, but partly also by temper, accustomed to have dirty clothes and dirty hands normally and without discomfort. He regards cleanliness as a kind of

The Other Kind of Man

separate and special costume ; to be put on for great festivals. He has several really curious characteristics, which would attract the eyes of sociologists, if they had any eyes. For instance, his vocabulary is coarse and abusive, in marked contrast to his actual spirit, which is generally patient and civil. He has an odd way of using certain words of really horrible meaning, but using them quite innocently and without the most distant taint of the evils to which they allude. He is rather sentimental; and, like most sentimental people, not devoid of snobbishness. At the same time, he believes the ordinary manly commonplaces of freedom and fraternity as he believes most of the decent traditions of Christian men : he finds it very difficult to act according to them, but this difficulty is not confined to him. He has a strong and individual sense of humour, and not much power of corporate or militant action. He is not a Socialist. Finally, he bears no more resemblance to a Labour Member than he does to a City Alderman or a Die-Hard Duke. This is the Common Labourer of England ; and it is he who is on the march at last.

See this man in your mind as you see him in the street, realize that it is his open mind 22;

A Miscellany of Men

we wish to influence or his empty stomach we wish to cure, and then consider seriously (if you can) the five men, including two of his own alleged oppressors, who were summoned as a Royal Commission to consider his claims when he or his sort went out on strike upon the railways. I knew nothing against, indeed I knew nothing about, any of the gentlemen then summoned, beyond a bare introduction to Mr. Henderson, whom I liked, but whose identity I was in no danger of confusing with that of a railway-porter. I do not think that any old gentleman, however absent-minded, would be likely on arriving at Euston, let us say, to hand his Gladstone-bag to Mr. Henderson or to attempt to reward that politician with twopence. Of the others I can only judge by the facts about their status as set forth in the public Press. The Chairman, Sir David Har-rell, appeared to be an ex-official distinguished in (of all things in the world) the Irish Constabulary. I have no earthly reason to doubt that the Chairman meant to be fair ; but I am not talking about what men mean to be, but about what they are. The police in Ireland are practically an army of occupation ; a man serving in them or directing them is practically a soldier ; and, of course, he must do his 224

The Other Kind of Man

duty as such. But it seems truly extraordinary to select as one likely to sympathize with the democracy of England a man whose whole business in life it has been to govern against its will the democracy of Ireland. What should we say if Russian strikers were offered the sympathetic arbitration of the head of the Russian Police in Finland or Poland ? And if we do not know that the whole civilized world sees Ireland with Poland as a typical oppressed nation, it is time we did. The Chairman, whatever his personal virtues, must be by instinct and habit akin to the capitalists in the dispute. Two more of the Commissioners actually were the capitalists in the dispute. Then came Mr. Henderson (pushing his trolley and cheerily crying, " By your leave "), and then another less known gentleman who had " corresponded " with the Board of Trade, and had thus gained some strange claim to represent the very poor.

Now people like this might quite possibly produce a rational enough report, and in this or that respect even improve things. Men of that kind are tolerably kind, tolerably patriotic, and tolerably business-like. But if any one supposes that men of that kind can conceivably quiet any real quarrel with the 15 225

A Miscellany of Men

Man of the Other Kind, the man whom I first described, it is frantic. The common worker is angry exactly because he has found out that all these boards consist of the same well-dressed Kind of Man, whether they are called Governmental or Capitalist. If any one hopes that he will reconcile the poor, I say, as I said at the beginning, that such a one has not looked on the light of day or dwelt in the land of the living.

But I do not criticize such a Commission except for one most practical and urgent purpose. It will be answered to me that the first Kind of Man of whom I spoke could not really be on boards and committees, as modern England is managed. His dirt, though necessary and honourable, would be offensive : his speech, though rich and figurative, would be almost incomprehensible. Let us grant, for the moment, that this is so. This Kind of Man, with his sooty hair or sanguinary adjectives, cannot be represented at our committees of arbitration. Therefore, the other Kind of Man, fairly prosperous, fairly plausible, at home at least with the middle class, capable at least of reaching and touching the upper class, he must remain the only Kind of Man for such councils.

The Other Kind of Man

Very well. If, then, you give at any future time any kind of compulsory powers to such councils to prevent strikes, you will be driving the first Kind of Man to work for a particular master as much as if you drove him with a whip.

The Mediaeval Villain

I SEE that there have been more attempts at the whitewashing ot King John. But the gentleman who wrote has a further t interest in the matter; for he believes that King John was innocent, not only on this point, but as a whole. He thinks King John has been very badly treated ; though I am not sure whether he would attribute to that Plantagenet a saintly merit or merely a humdrum respectability.

I sympathize with the whitewashing of King John, merely because it is a protest against our waxwork style of history. Everybody is in a particular attitude, with particular moral attributes; Rufus is always hunting and Coeur-de-Lion always crusading ; Henry VIII always marrying, and Charles I always having his head cut off; Alfred rapidly and in rotation making his people's 228

The Mediaeval Villain

clocks and spoiling their cakes ; and King John pulling out Jews' teeth with the celerity and industry of an American dentist. Anything is good that shakes all this stiff simplification, and makes us remember that these men were once alive ; that is, mixed, free, flippant, and inconsistent. It gives the mind a healthy kick to know that Alfred had fits, that Charles I prevented enclosures, that Rufus was really interested in architecture, that Henry VIII was really interested in theology.

And as these scraps of reality can startle us into more solid imagination of events, so can even errors and exaggerations if they are on the right side. It does some good to call Alfred a prig, Charles I a Puritan, and John a jolly good fellow ; if this makes us feel that they were people whom we might have liked or disliked. I do not myself think that John was a nice gentleman ; but for all that the popular picture of him is all wrong. Whether he had any generous qualities or not, he had what commonly makes them possible, dare-devil courage, for instance, and hot-headed decision. But, above all, he had a morality which he broke, but which we misunderstand.

A Miscellany of Men

The mediaeval mind turned centrally upon the pivot of Free Will. In their social system the medisevals were too much parti-per-pale, as their heralds would say, too rigidly cut up by fences and quarterings of guild or degree. But in their moral philosophy they always thought of man as standing free and doubtful at the cross-roads in a forest. While they clad and bound the body and (to some extent) the mind too stiffly and quaintly for our taste, they had a much stronger sense than we have of the freedom of the soul. For them the soul always hung poised like an eagle in the heavens of liberty. Many of the things that strike a modern as most fantastic came from their keen sense of the power of choice.

For instance, the greatest of the Schoolmen devotes folios to the minute description of what the world would have been like if Adam had refused the apple; what kings, laws, babies, animals, planets would have been in an unfallen world. So intensely does he feel that Adam might have decided the other way that he sees a complete and complex vision of another world, a world that now can never be.

This sense of the stream of life in a man that may turn either way can be felt through all their popular ethics in legend, chronicle, 230

The Mediaeval Villain

and ballad. It is a feeling which has been weakened among us by two heavy intellectual forces. The Calvinism of the seventeenth century and the physical science of the nineteenth, whatever other truths they may have taught, have darkened this liberty with a sense of doom. We think of bad men as something like black men, a separate and incurable kind of people. The Byronic spirit was really a sort of operatic Calvinism. It brought the villain upon the stage ; the lost soul; the modern version of King John. But the contemporaries of King John did not feel like that about him, even when they detested him. They instinctively felt him to be a man of mixed passions like themselves, who was allowing his evil passions to have much too good a time of it. They might have spoken of him as a man in considerable danger of going to hell ; but they would not have talked of him as if he had come from there. In the ballads of Percy or Robin Hood it frequently happens that the King comes upon the scene, and his ultimate decision makes the climax of the tale. But we do not feel, as we do in the Byronic or modern romance, that there is a definite stage direction " Enter Tyrant." Nor do we behold a deus ex machina who is certain 231

A Miscellany of Men

to do all that is mild and just. The King in the ballad is in a state of virile indecision. Sometimes he will pass from a towering passion to the most sweeping magnanimity and friendliness ; sometimes he will begin an act of vengeance and be turned from it by a jest. Yet this august levity is not moral indifference ; it is moral freedom. It is the strong sense in the writer that the King, being the type of man with power, will probably sometimes use it badly and sometimes well. In this sense John is certainly misrepresented, for he is pictured as something that none of his own friends or enemies saw. In that sense he was certainly not so black as he is painted, for he lived in a world where every one was piebald.

King John would be represented in a modern play or novel as a kind of degenerate ; a shifty-eyed moral maniac with a twist in his soul's backbone and green blood in his veins. The mediaevals were quite capable of boiling him in melted lead, but they would have been quite incapable of despairing of his soul in the modern fashion. A striking a fortiori case is that of the strange mediaeval legend of Robert the Devil. Robert was represented as a mon-232

strous birth sent to an embittered woman actually in answer to prayers to Satan, and his earlier actions are simply those of the infernal fire let loose upon earth. But though he can be called almost literally a child of hell, yet the climax of the story is his repentance at Rome and his great reparation. That is the paradox of mediaeval morals, as it must appear to the moderns. We must try to conceive a race of men who hated John, and sought his blood, and believed every abomination about him, who would have been quite capable of assassinating or torturing him in the extremity of their anger. And yet we must admit that they would not really have been fundamentally surprised if he had shaved his head in humiliation, given all his goods to the poor, embraced the lepers in a lazar-house, and been canonized as a saint in heaven. So strongly did they hold that the pivot of Will should turn freely, which now is rusted, and sticks.

For we, whatever our political opinions, certainly never think of our public men like that. If we hold the opinion that Mr. Lloyd George is a noble tribune of the populace and protector of the poor, we do not admit that he can ever have paltered with the truth or bar-

gained with the powerful. If we hold the equally idiotic opinion that he is a red and rabid Socialist, maddening mobs into mutiny and theft, then we expect him to go on maddening them— and us. We do not expect him, let us say, suddenly to go into a monastery. We have lost the idea of repentance ; especially in public things ; that is why we cannot really get rid of our great national abuses of economic tyranny and aristocratic avarice. Progress in the modern sense is a very dismal drudge ; and mostly consists of being moved on by the police. We move on because we are not allowed to move back. But the really ragged prophets, the real revolutionists who held high language in the palaces of kings, they did not confine themselves to saying, " Onward, Christian soldiers," still less, " Onward, Futurist soldiers " ; what they said to high emperors and to whole empires was, " Turn ye, turn ye, why will ye die ? "

V The Divine Detective ^> *^> *o *^x

1 " VERY person of sound education enjoys l^ detective stories, and there are even several points on which they have a hearty superiority to most modern books. A detective story generally describes six living men discussing how it is that a man is dead. A modern philosophic story generally describes six dead men discussing how any man can possibly be alive. But those who have enjoyed the roman policier must have noted one thing, that when the murderer is caught he is hardly ever hanged. " That," says Sherlock Holmes, " is the advantage of being a private detective " ; after he has caught he can set free. The Christian Church can best be denned as an enormous private detective, correcting that official detective-—the State. This, indeed, is one of the injustices done to historic Christianity ; injustices which arise from looking at complex exceptions and not at the large and simple fact. We are constantly being told that theologians used racks and thumbscrews, and so they did. Theologians used racks and

thumbscrews just as they used thimbles and three-legged stools, because everybody else used them. Christianity no more created the mediaeval tortures than it did the Chinese tortures ; it inherited them from any empire as heathen as the Chinese.

The Church did, in an evil hour, consent to imitate the commonwealth and employ cruelty. But if we open our eyes and take in the whole picture, if we look at the general shape and colour of the thing, the real difference between the Church and the State is huge and plain. The State, in all lands and ages, has created a machinery of punishment, more bloody and brutal in some places than others, but bloody and brutal everywhere. The Church is the only institution that ever attempted to create a machinery of pardon. The Church is the only thing that ever attempted by system to pursue and discover crimes, not in order to avenge, but in order to forgive them. The stake and rack were merely the weaknesses of the religion; its snobberies, its surrenders to the world. Its speciality——or, if you like, its oddity —was this merciless mercy; the unrelenting sleuthhound who seeks to save and not slay.

The Divine Detective

I can best illustrate what I mean by referring to two popular plays on somewhat parallel topics, which have been successful here and in America. The Passing of the Third Floor Back is a humane and reverent experiment, dealing with the influence of one unknown but divine figure as he passes through a group of squalid characters. I have no desire to make cheap fun of the extremely abrupt conversions of all these people ; that is a point of art, not of morals ; and, after all, many conversions have been abrupt. This saviour's method of making people good is to tell them how good they are already ; and in the case of suicidal outcasts, whose moral backs are broken, and who are soaked with sincere self-contempt, I can imagine that this might be quite the right way. I should not deliver this message to authors or members of Parliament, because they would so heartily agree with it.

Still, it is not altogether here that I differ from the moral of Mr. Jerome's play. I differ vitally from his story because it is not a detective story. There is in it none of this great Christian idea of tearing their evil out of men ; it lacks the realism of the saints. Redemption should bring truth as well as peace ; and truth is a fine thing, though the materialists did'go 237

A Miscellany of Men

mad about it. Things must be faced, even in order to be forgiven ; the great objection to " letting sleeping dogs lie " is that they lie in more senses than one. But in Mr. Jerome's Passing of the Third Floor Back the redeemer is not a divine detective, pitiless in his resolve to know and pardon. Rather he is a sort of divine dupe, who does not pardon at all, because he does not see anything that is going on. It may, or may not, be true to say, " Tout comprendre est tout pardonner." But it is much more evidently true to say, " Rien comprendre est rien pardonner," and the " Third Floor Back" does not seem to comprehend anything. He might, after all, be a quite selfish sentimentalist, who found it comforting to think well of his neighbours. There is nothing very heroic in loving after you have been deceived. The heroic business is to love after you have been undeceived.

When I saw this play it was natural to compare it with another play which I had not seen, but which I have read in its printed version. I mean Mr. Rann Kennedy's Servant in the House the success of which sprawls over so many of the American news-238

The Divine Detective

papers. This also is concerned with a dim, yet evidently divine, figure changing the destinies of a whole group of persons. It is a better play structurally than the other ; in fact, it is a very fine play indeed ; but there is nothing aesthetic or fastidious about it. It is as much or more than the other sensational, democratic, and (I use the word in a sound and good sense) Salvationist.

But the difference lies precisely in this'— that the Christ of Mr. Kennedy's play insists on really knowing all the souls that he loves ; he declines to conquer by a kind of supernatural stupidity. He pardons evil, but he will not ignore it. In other words, he is a Christian, and not a Christian Scientist. The distinction doubtless is partly explained by the problems severally selected. Mr. Jerome practically supposes Christ to be trying to save disreputable people ; and that, of course, is naturally a simple business. Mr. Kennedy supposes Him to be trying to save the reputable people, which is a much larger affair. The chief characters in The Servant in the House are a popular and strenuous vicar, universally respected, and his fashionable and forcible wife. It would have been no good to tell these people they had some good in them

•—for that was what they were telling themselves all day long. They had to be reminded that they had some bad in them-—instinctive idolatries and silent treasons which they always tried to forget. It is in connexion with these crimes of wealth and culture that we face the real problem of positive evil. The whole of Mr. Blatchford's controversy about sin was vitiated throughout by one's consciousness that whenever he wrote the word " sinner " he thought of a man in rags. But here, again, we can find truth merely by referring to vulgar literature—its unfailing fountain. Whoever read a detective story about poor people ? The poor have crimes ; but the poor have no secrets. And it is because the proud have secrets that they need to be detected before they are forgiven.

The Elf of Japan ^> ^> ^> ^> ^>

THERE are things in this world of which I can say seriously that I love them but I do not like them. The point is not merely verbal, but psychologically quite valid. Cats are the first things that occur to me as examples of the principle. Cats are so beautiful that a creature from another star might fall in love with them, and so incalculable that he might kill them. Some of my friends take quite a high moral line about cats. Some, like Mr. Titterton, I think, admire a cat for its moral independence and readiness to scratch anybody "if he does not behave himself." Others, like Mr. Belloc, regard the cat as cruel and secret, a fit friend for witches ; one who will devour everything, except, indeed, poisoned food, " so utterly lacking is it in Christian simplicity and humility." For my part, I have neither of these feelings. I admire cats as I admire catkins ; those little fluffy things that hang on trees. They are both pretty and both furry, and both declare 16 241

the glory of God. And this abstract exultation in all living things is truly to be called Love ; for it is a higher feeling than mere affectional convenience ; it is a vision. It is heroic, and even saintly, in this : that it asks for nothing in return. I love all the cats in the street as St. Francis of Assisi loved all the birds in the wood or all the fishes in the sea ; not so much, of course, but then I am not a saint. But he did not wish to bridle a bird and ride on its back, as one bridles and rides on a horse. He did not wish to put a collar round a fish's neck, marked with the name " Francis," and the address " Assisi "•—as one does with a dog. He did not wish them to belong to him or himself to belong to them ; in fact, it would be a very awkward experience to belong to a lot of fishes. But a man does belong to his dog, in another but an equally real sense with that in which the dog belongs to him. The two bonds of obedience and responsibility vary very much with the dogs and the men ; but they are both bonds. In other words, a man does not merely love a dog ; as he might (in a mystical moment) love any sparrow that perched on his window-sill or any rabbit that ran across his path. A man likes a dog ; and that is a serious matter. 242

The Elf of Japan

To me, unfortunately perhaps (for I speak merely of individual taste), a cat is a wild animal. A cat is Nature personified. Like Nature, it is so mysterious that one cannot quite repose even in its beauty. But like Nature again, it is so beautiful that one cannot believe that it is really cruel. Perhaps it isn't; and there again it is like Nature. Men of old time worshipped cats as they worshipped crocodiles ; and those magnificent old mystics knew what they were about. The moment in which one really loves cats is the same as that in which one (moderately and within reason) loves crocodiles. It is that divine instant when a man feels himself-—no, not absorbed into the unity of all things (a loathsome fancy) •—but delighting in the difference of all things. At the moment when a man really knows he is a man he will feel, however faintly, a kind of fairy-tale pleasure in the fact that a crocodile is a crocodile. All the more will he exult in the things that are more evidently beautiful than crocodiles, such as flowers and birds and cats — which are more beautiful than either. But it does not follow that he will wish to pick all the flowers or to cage all the birds or to own all the cats.

No one who still believes in democracy and

A Miscellany of Men

the rights of man will admit that any division between men and men can be anything but a fanciful analogy to the division between men and animals. But in the sphere of such fanciful analogy there are even human beings whom I feel to be like cats in this respect: that I can love them without liking them. I feel it about certain quaint and alien societies, especially about the Japanese. The exquisite old Japanese draughtsmanship (of which we shall see no more, now Japan has gone in for Progress and Imperialism) had a quality that was infinitely attractive and intangible. Japanese pictures were really rather like pictures made by cats. They were full of feathery softness and of sudden and spirited scratches. If any one will wander in some gallery fortunate enough to have a fine collection of those slight water-colour sketches on rice paper which come from the remote East, he will observe many elements in them which a fanciful person might consider feline. There is, for instance, that odd enjoyment of the tops of trees ; those airy traceries of forks and fading twigs, up to which certainly no artist, but only a cat could climb. There is that elvish love of the full moon, as large and lucid as a Chinese lantern, hung in these tenuous 244

The Elf of Japan

branches. That moon is so large and luminous that one can imagine a hundred cats howling under it. Then there is the exhaustive treatment of the anatomy of birds and fish; subjects in which cats are said to be interested. Then there is the slanting cat-like eye of all these Eastern gods and men—but this is getting altogether too coincident. We shall have another racial theory in no time (beginning " Are the Japs Cats ? "), and though I shall not believe in my theory, somebody else might. There are people among my esteemed correspondents who might believe anything. It is enough for me to say here that in this small respect Japs affect me like cats. I mean that I love them. I love their quaint and native poetry, their instinct of easy civilization, their unique unreplaceable art, the testimony they bear to the bustling, irrepressible activities of nature and man. If I were a real mystic looking down on them from a real mountain, I am sure I should love them more even than the strong-winged and unwearied birds or the fruitful, ever-multiplying fish. But, as for liking them, as one likes a dog'—that is quite another matter. That would mean trusting them.

In the old English and Scotch ballads the 245

fairies are regarded very much in the way that I feel inclined to regard Japs and cats. They are not specially spoken of as evil ; they are enjoyed as witching and wonderful; but they are not trusted as good. You do not say the wrong words or give the wrong gifts to them ; and there is a curious silence about what would happen to you if you did. Now to me, Japan, the Japan of Art, was always a fairyland. What trees as gay as flowers and peaks as white as wedding cakes ; what lanterns as large as houses and houses as frail as lanterns ! . . . but . . . but . . . the missionary explained (I read in the paper) that the assertion and denial about the Japanese use of torture was a mere matter of verbal translation. " The Japanese would not call twisting the thumbs back ' torture .' "

The Chartered Libertine ^> ^ ^>

I FIND myself in agreement with Mr. Robert Lynd for his most just remark in connexion with the Malatesta case, that the police are becoming a peril to society. I have no attraction to that sort of atheist asceticism to which the purer types of Anarchism tend ; but both an atheist and an ascetic are better men than a spy ; and it is ignominious to see one's country thus losing her special point of honour about asylum and liberty. It will be quite a new departure if we begin to protect and whitewash foreign policemen. I always understood it was only English policemen who were absolutely spotless. A good many of us, however, have begun to feel with Mr. Lynd, and on all sides authorities and officials are being questioned. But there is one most graphic and extraordinary fact, which it did not lie in Mr. Lynd's way to touch upon, but which somebody really must seize and emphasize. It is this : that at the very time when we are all beginning to doubt these authorities, we 247

are letting laws pass to increase their most capricious powers. All our commissions, petitions, and letters to the papers are asking whether these authorities can give an account of their stewardship. And at the same moment all our laws are decreeing that they shall not give any account of their stewardship, but shall become yet more irresponsible stewards. Bills like the Feeble-Minded Bill and the Inebriate Bill (very appropriate names for them) actually arm with scorpions the hand that has chastised the Malatestas and Maleckas with whips. The inspector, the doctor, the police sergeant, the well-paid person who writes certificates and " passes " this, that, or the other ; this sort of man is being trusted with more authority, apparently because he is being doubted with more reason. In one room we are asking why the Government and the great experts between them cannot sail a ship. In another room we are deciding that the Government and experts shall be allowed, without trial or discussion, to immure any one's bo_dy, damn any one's soul, and dispose of unborn generations with the levity of a pagan god. We are putting the official on the throne while he is still in the dock.

The Chartered Libertine

The mere meaning of words is now strangely forgotten and falsified ; as when people talk of an author's " message," without thinking whom it is from ; and I have noted in these connexions the strange misuse of another word. It is the excellent mediaeval word " charter." I remember the Act that sought to save gutter-boys from cigarettes was called " The Children's Charter." Similarly the Act which seeks to lock up as lunatics people who are not lunatics was actually called a " charter " of the feeble-minded. Now this terminology is insanely wrong, even if the Bills are right. Even were they right in theory they would be applied only to the poor, like many better rules about education and cruelty. A woman was lately punished for cruelty because her children were not washed when it was proved that she had no water. From that it will be an easy step in Advanced Thought to punishing a man for wine-bibbing when it is proved that he had no wine. Rifts in right reason widen down the ages. And when we have begun by shutting up a confessedly kind person for cruelty, we may yet come to shutting up Mr. Tom Mann for feeblemindedness.

But even if such laws do good to children or 249

A Miscellany of Men

idiots, it is wrong to use the word " charter." A charter does not mean a thing that does good to people. It means a thing that grants people more rights and liberties. It may be a good thing for gutter-boys to be deprived of their cigarettes : it might be a good thing for aldermen to be deprived of their cigars. But I think the Goldsmiths' Company would be very much surprised if the King granted them a new charter (in place of their mediaeval charter), and it only meant that policemen might pull the cigars out of their mouths. It may be a good thing that all drunkards should be locked up : and many acute statesmen (King John, for instance) would certainly have thought it a good thing if all aristocrats could be locked up. But even that somewhat cynical prince would scarcely have granted to the barons a thing called " the Great Charter " and then locked them all up on the strength of it. If he had, this interpretation of the word " charter " would have struck the barons with considerable surprise. I doubt if their narrow mediaeval minds could have taken it in.

The roots of the real England are in the early Middle Ages, and no Englishman will 250

The Chartered Libertine

ever understand his own language (or even his own conscience) till he understands them. And he will never understand them till he understands this word " charter." I will attempt in a moment to state in older, more suitable terms, what a charter was. In modern, practical and political terms, it is quite easy to state what a charter was. A charter was the thing that the railway workers wanted last Christmas and did not get ; and apparently will never get. It is called in the current jargon " recognition " ; the acknowledgment in so many words by society of the immunities or freedoms of a certain set of men. If there had been railways in the Middle Ages there would probably have been a railwaymen's guild ; and it would have had a charter from the King, denning their rights. A charter is the expression of an idea still true and then almost universal : that authority is necessary for nothing so much as for the granting of liberties. Like everything mediaeval, it ramified back to a root in religion ; and was a sort of small copy of the Christian idea of man's creation. Man was free, not because there was no God, but because it needed a God to set him free. By authority he was free. By authority the craftsmen of the guilds were free. Many 251

A Miscellany of Men

other great philosophers took and take the other view : the Lucretian pagans, the Moslem fatalists, the modern monists and determinists, all roughly confine themselves to saying that God gave man a law. The mediaeval Christian insisted that God gave man a charter. Modern feeling may not sympathize with its list of liberties, which included the liberty to be damned ; but that has nothing to do with the fact that it was a gift of liberties and not of laws. This was mirrored, however dimly, in the whole system. There was a great deal of gross inequality ; and in other aspects absolute equality was taken for granted. But the point is that equality and inequality were ranks—— or rights. There were not only things one was forbidden to do ; but things one was forbidden to forbid. A man was not only definitely responsible, but definitely irresponsible. The holidays of his soul were immovable feasts. All a charter really meant lingers alive in that poetic phrase that calls the wind a " chartered " libertine.

Lie awake at night and hear the wind blowing ; hear it knock at every man's door and shout down every man's chimney. Feel how it takes liberties with everything, having taken primary liberty for itself ; feel that the

The Chartered Libertine

wind is always a vagabond and sometimes almost a housebreaker. But remember that in the days when free men had charters, they held that the wind itself was wild by authority; and was only free because it had a father.

The Contented Man ^> ^> ^> ^>

r I "HE word content is not inspiring now-_L adays; rather it is irritating because it is dull. It prepares the mind for a little sermon in the style of the Vicar of Wakefield about how you and I should be satisfied with our countrified innocence and our simple village sports. The word, however, has two meanings, somewhat singularly connected; the " sweet content " of the poet and the " cubic content " of the mathematician. Some distinguish these by stressing the different syllables. Thus, it might happen to any of us, at some social juncture, to remark gaily, " Of the content of the King of the Cannibal Islands' Stewpot I am content to be ignorant " ; or " Not content with measuring the cubic content of my safe, you are stealing the spoons." And there really is an analogy between the mathematical and the moral use of the term, for lack of the observation of which the latter has been much weakened and misused.

The Contented Man

The preaching of contentment is in disrepute, well deserved in so far that the moral is really quite inapplicable to the anarchy and insane peril of our tall and toppling cities. Content suggests some kind of security ; and it is not strange that our workers should often think about rising above their position, since they have so continually to think about sinking below it. The philanthropist who urges the poor to saving and simple pleasures deserves all the derision that he gets. To advise people to be content with what they have got may or may not be sound moral philosophy.

But to urge people to be content with what they haven't got is a piece of impudence hard for even the English poor to pardon. But though the creed of content is unsuited to certain special riddles and wrongs, it remains true for the normal of mortal life. We speak of divine discontent; discontent may sometimes be a divine thing, but content must always be the human thing. It may be true that a particular man, in his relation to his master or his neighbour, to his country or his enemies, will do well to be fiercely unsatisfied or thirsting for an angry justice. But it is not true, no sane person can call it true, that man as a whole in his general attitude

A Miscellany of Men

towards the world, in his posture towards death or green fields, towards the weather or the baby, will be wise to cultivate dissatisfaction. In a broad estimate of our earthly experience, the great truism on the tablet remains : he must not covet his neighbour's ox nor his ass nor anything that is his. In highly complex and scientific civilizations he may sometimes find himself forced into an exceptional vigilance. But, then, in highly complex and scientific civilizations, nine times out of ten, he only wants his own ass back.

But I wish to urge the case for cubic content; in which (even more than in moral content) I take a personal interest. Now, moral content has been undervalued and neglected because of its separation from the other meaning. It has become a negative rather than a positive thing. In some accounts of contentment it seems to be little more than a meek despair.

But this is not the true meaning of the term ; it should stand for the idea of a positive and thorough appreciation of the content of anything ; for feeling the substance and not merely the surface of experience. " Content " 256

The Contented Man

ought to mean in English, as it does in French, being pleased ; placidly, perhaps, but still positively pleased. Being contented with bread and cheese ought not to mean not caring what you eat. It ought to mean caring for bread and cheese ; handling and enjoying the cubic content of the bread and cheese and adding it to your own. Being content with an attic ought not to mean being unable to move from it and resigned to living in it. It ought to mean appreciating what there is to appreciate in such a position ; such as the quaint and elvish slope of the ceiling or the sublime aerial view of the opposite chimney - pots. And in this sense contentment is a real and even an active virtue ; it is not only affirmative, but creative. The poet in the attic does not forget the attic in poetic musings ; he remembers whatever the attic has of poetry ; he realizes how high, how starry, how cool, how unadorned and simple—in short, how Attic is the attic.

True contentment is a thing as active as agriculture. It is the power of getting out of any situation all that there is in it. It is arduous and it is rare. The absence of this digestive talent is what makes so cold and incredible the tales of so many people who 17 257

A Miscellany of Men

say they have been " through " things ; when it is evident that they have come out on the other side quite unchanged. A man might have gone " through " a plum pudding as a bullet might go through a plum pudding ; it depends on the size of the pudding—— and the man. But the awful and sacred question is " Has the pudding been through him ? " Has he tasted, appreciated, and absorbed the solid pudding, with its three dimensions and its three thousand tastes and smells ? Can he offer himself to the eyes of men as one who has cubically conquered and contained a pudding ?

In the same way we may ask of those who profess to have passed through trivial or tragic experiences whether they have absorbed the content of them ; whether they licked up such living water as there was. It is a pertinent question in connexion with many modern problems.

Thus the young genius says, " I have lived
in my dreary and squalid village before I
found success in Paris or Vienna." The sound
philosopher will answer, " You have never
The Contented Man
lived in your village, or you would not call it dreary and squalid."

Thus the Imperialist, the Colonial idealist (who commonly speaks and always thinks with a Yankee accent) will say, " I've been right away from these little muddy islands, and seen God's great seas and prairies." The sound philosopher will reply, " You have never been in these islands ; you have never seen the weald of Sussex or the plain of Salisbury ; otherwise you could never have called them either muddy or little."

Thus the Suffragette will say, " I have passed through the paltry duties of pots and pans, the drudgery of the vulgar kitchen ; but I have come out to intellectual liberty." The sound philosopher will answer, " You have never passed through the kitchen, or you never would call it vulgar. Wiser and stronger women than you have really seen a poetry in pots and pans ; naturally, because there is a poetry in them." It is right for the village violinist to climb into fame in Paris or Vienna ; it is right for the stray Englishman to climb across the high shoulder of the world ; it is right for the woman to climb into whatever cathedrae or high places she can allow to her sexual dignity. But it is wrong that any of 259

these climbers should kick the ladder by which they have climbed. But indeed these bitter people who record their experiences really record their lack of experiences. It is the countryman who has not succeeded in being a countryman who comes up to London. It is the clerk who has not succeeded in being a clerk who tries (on vegetarian principles) to be a countryman. And the woman with a past is generally a woman angry about the past she never had.

When you have really exhausted an experience you always reverence and love it. The two things that nearly all of us have thoroughly and really been through are childhood and youth. And though we would not have them back again on any account, we feel that they are both beautiful, because we have drunk them dry.

The Angry Author: His Farewell

I HAVE republished all these old articles of mine because they cover a very controversial period, in w r hich I was in nearly all the controversies, whether I was visible there or no. And I wish to gather up into this last article a valedictory violence about all such things ; and then pass to where, beyond these voices, there is peace——or in other words, to the writing of Penny Dreadfuls ; a noble and much-needed work. But before I finally desert the illusions of rationalism for the actualities of romance, I should very much like to write one last roaring, raging book telling all the rationalists not to be so utterly irrational. The book would be simply a string of violent vetoes, like the Ten Commandments. I would call it " Don'ts for Dogmatists ; or Things I am Tired Of."

This book of intellectual etiquette, like most books of etiquette, would begin with superficial things ; but there would be, I fancy, a wailing

imprecation in the words that could not be called artificial ; it might begin thus :—

(1) Don't use a noun and then an adjective that crosses out the noun. An adjective qualifies, it cannot contradict. Don't say, " Give me a patriotism that is free from all boundaries." It is like saying, " Give me a pork pie with no pork in it." Don't say, " I look forward to that larger religion that shall have no special dogmas." It is like saying, " I look forward to that larger quadruped who shall have no feet." A quadruped means something with four feet; and a religion means something that commits a man to some doctrine about the universe. Don't let the meek substantive be absolutely murdered by the joyful, exuberant adjective.

(2) Don't say you are not going to say a thing, and then say it. This practice is very flourishing and successful with public speakers. The trick consists of first repudiating a certain view in unfavourable terms, and then repeating the same view in favourable terms. Perhaps the simplest form of it may be found in a landlord of my neighbourhood, who said to his tenants in an election speech, " Of course I'm not going to threaten you, but if this Budget passes the rents

will go up." The

thing can be done in many forms besides this. " I am the last man to mention party politics ; but when I see the Empire rent in pieces by irresponsible Radicals," etc. " In this hall we welcome all creeds, We have no hostility against any honest belief ; but only against that black priestcraft and superstition which can accept such a doctrine as," etc. " I would not say one word that could ruffle our relations with Germany. But this I will say ; that when I see ceaseless and unscrupulous armament," etc. Please don't do it. Decide to make a remark or not to make a remark. But don't fancy that you have somehow softened the saying of a thing by having just promised not to say it.

(3) Don't use secondary words as primary words. " Happiness " (let us say) is a primary word. You know when you have the thing, and you jolly well know when you haven't. " Progress " is a secondary word ; it means the degree of one's approach to happiness, or to some such solid ideal. But modern controversies constantly turn on asking, " Does Happiness help Progress ? " Thus, I see in the New Age this week a letter from Mr. Egerton Swann, in which he warns the world against me and my friend Mr. 263

Belloc, on the ground that our democracy is "spasmodic" (whatever that means); while our " reactionism is settled and permanent." It never strikes Mr. Swann that democracy means something in itself ; while " reactionism " means nothing—except in connexion with democracy. You cannot react except from something. If Mr. Swann thinks I have ever reacted from the doctrine that the people should rule, I wish he would give me the reference.

(4) Don't say, " There is no true creed ; for each creed believes itself right and the others wrong." Probably one of the creeds is right and the others are wrong. Diversity does show that most. of the views must be wrong. It does not by the faintest logic show that they all must be wrong. I suppose there is no subject on which opinions differ with more desperate sincerity than about which horse will win the Derby. These are certainly solemn convictions ; men risk ruin for them. The man who puts his shirt on Potosi must believe in that animal, and each of the other men putting their last garments upon other quadrupeds must believe in them quite as sincerely. They are all serious, and most of them are wrong. But one of them is right. One of the faiths 264

is justified; one of the horses does win; not always even the dark horse which might stand for Agnosticism, but often the obvious and popular horse of Orthodoxy. Democracy has its occasional victories ; and even the Favourite has been known to come in first.

But the point here is that something comes in first. That there were many beliefs does not destroy the fact that there was one well-founded belief. I believe (merely upon authority) that the world is round. That there may be tribes who believe it to be triangular or oblong does not alter the fact that it is certainly some shape, and therefore not any other shape. Therefore I repeat, with the wail of imprecation, don't say that the variety of creeds prevents you from accepting any creed. It is an unintelligent remark.

(5) Don't (if any one calls your doctrine mad, which is likely enough), don't answer that madmen are only the minority and the sane only the majority. The sane are sane because they are the corporate substance of mankind ; the insane are not a minority because they are not a mob. The man who thinks himself a man thinks the next man a man ; he reckons his neighbour as himself. But the man who thinks he is a chicken does not try to look 265

through the man who thinks he is glass. The man who thinks himself Jesus Christ does not quarrel with the man who thinks himself Rockefeller; as would certainly happen if the two had ever met. But madmen never meet. It is the only thing they cannot do. They can talk, they can inspire, they can fight, they can found religions ; but they cannot meet. Maniacs can never be the majority ; for the simple reason that they can never be even a minority. If two madmen had ever agreed they might have conquered the world.

(6) Don't say that the idea of human equality is absurd, because some men are tall and some short, some, clever and some stupid. At the height of the French Revolution it was noticed that Danton was tall and Marat short. In the wildest popular excitement of America it is known that Rockefeller is stupid and that Bryan is clever. The doctrine of human equality reposes upon this. That there is no man really clever who has not found that he is stupid. That there is no big man who has not felt small. Some men never feel small ; but these are the few men who are.

(7) Don't say (O don't say) that Primitive Man knocked down a woman with a club and carried her away. Why on earth should he ?

The Angry Author : His Farewell

Does the male sparrow knock down the female sparrow with a twig ? Does the male giraffe knock down the female giraffe with a palm tree ? Why should the male have had to use any violence at any time in order to make the female a female ? Why should the woman roll herself in the mire lower than the sow or the she-bear ; and profess to have been a slave where all these creatures were creators ; where all these beasts were gods ? Do not talk such bosh. I implore you, I supplicate you not to talk such bosh. Utterly and absolutely abolish all such bosh——and we may yet begin to discuss these public questions properly. But I fear my list of protests grows too long ; and I know it could grow longer for ever. The reader must forgive my elongations and elaborations. I fancied for the moment that I was writing a book.

PRINTED BY
WILLIAM BRENDON AND SON. LTD. PLYMOUTH
JULY 1912 A FEW OF
MESSRS. METHUEN'S
PUBLICATIONS
THE END

First Published in 1912

Made in the USA
Middletown, DE
08 January 2021